The Lonely Heart Attack Club

J C Williams

ISBN-10: 1548766429

ISBN-13: 978-1548766429

First printing July 2017

Second printing October 2018

Third printing January 2020

Cover artwork by Paul Nugent

Formatting & interior design provided by Dave Scott and Cupboardy Wordsmithing

Chapter One

Jack thumbed through the discarded pile of letters strewn in the entrance hall. *Rubbish, rubbish, junk...* He recognised one which he opened in frustration.

"Grandad, you have to open your post! There's one from the hospital. Great... your blood appointment was yesterday. Grandad..."

Jack took a dated-looking floral air spray which sat on the hall table and applied it liberally as he moved through the bungalow. The scent was overpowering and thick. He grimaced as it filled the air, sticking to his clothes. A thin film of rust at the base of the tin indicated it was past its best, but it served the purpose of removing the musty odour that hung in the air. Where did that old-person smell come from?

A rasping voice erupted from the living room, "Put that bloody tin away, Jack. It smells like a tart's bedroom!"

Jack ignored it, giving one final burst as he walked towards the threadbare fabric armchair positioned inches from the television.

"How did you know it was me?" he said, placing a kiss on the top of his grandad's head. "And how would you know what a tart's bedroom smells like?"

Jack reached across his chair and turned the volume down. "Why do you sit in this bloody chair? You've got a perfectly good sofa there. This thing is falling apart."

1

His grandad, Geoffrey, dismissed him with the flick of his hand.

"Here, Jack!" he said, as he forced himself out of his chair with vigour.

He was smart, exceptionally so. Jack was slightly taken aback as his grandad tucked his blue-checked shirt into his dark grey trousers. He pointed proudly at his immaculately polished leather shoes. He'd even had a haircut. The usual erratic white hair was neatly parted at the side, and for his age, he had a fine head of hair. He looked ten years younger.

"What do you think, Jack?"

"Have you got aftershave on?" asked Jack, moving his nose closer to his neck. "You have as well, you saucy old bugger! You're the one that smells like a tart's bedroom!"

Geoffrey shuffled nervously, like a child desperate to tell their parents they've been selected for the swimming gala.

"I've got a date!" he said, with a broad smile on his face.

Jack suppressed his first reaction as he could sense this was important. Grandad was eighty, and as far as the family knew, had shown no interest in women since his wife died.

Jack tilted his head slightly. "Oh… okay. Unexpected, but, okay… With who?"

"Sandra!" he said.

Jack stared blankly.

"Sandra Hardy… lives down by the shop. You know her! She's had a washing machine in her garden for years."

Jack didn't have a clue. Two thoughts ran through his head: figment of his imagination, or dating scam.

"That's nice… I'm pleased for you!" replied Jack, in an unintendedly condescending tone.

Geoffrey stomped towards the glass table and grabbed his wallet. He flicked through a small pile of notes and receipts, before thrusting a photograph an inch from Jack's face. It was too close to focus, so he took a step back. Jack took the picture from his hand.

He looked bewildered. "It's a topless photo, Grandad? I'm guessing that's... Sandra?"

The smile on his face confirmed the identity and as Jack's gaze ventured north of her considerable assets, he stared at her face. Jack knew exactly who it was.

"That's Sandy, Grandad! Not Sandra."

"That's what I said, Jack!"

"Grandad, that's... *Sandy!*"

Geoffrey scowled. "I know who it bloody is, Jack!"

Jack could see he was getting animated, and in view of his current blood pressure problems, thought better of pressing the point.

"You look smart, Grandad. Very smart! Just... just take care, okay? Mum said she would look in on you in the morning, and if you need me, just ring." Jack stood on an errant wire, and knew immediately what it was connected to — or *not* connected to, in this case. "Have you unplugged the soddin' phone again?"

Jack knelt and plugged the phone back into its socket. "You need to keep this in. What if we need to phone you?"

"No bugger of interest phones me, Jack."

"No, they won't, Grandad, and that's because you never plug the thing in! I need to get home. If you need me, just call, I can be here in five minutes. I'll drop by after work tomorrow. You can tell me all about your date. Oh, and phone the hospital to make another appointment. I've left you steak pie in the kitchen and some soup."

It was a balmy summer's evening and Jack took a moment to admire the perfectly manicured garden. A white gravel path ran from the front door to the knee-high white picket fence which adorned the neat bungalow. Vibrant flowers emerged from symmetrical wooden planters located under the windows. The garden was always the finest on the cul-de-sac. Until the death of his beloved, Val, he had the same sense of pride in his personal appearance, but this had waned. Jack was delighted to see him immaculately dressed, and he had a wry smile as he thought of the topless picture. How do I tell Mum, that he's got a date with... *Sandy?*

Jack climbed onto his ageing Vespa and looked in annoyance as the sun's rays amplified the rust on the once magnificent chrome mirrors. It was only a short ride to his flat on the outskirts of Onchan, about two miles from the Isle of Man's capital, Douglas. It wasn't the most convenient location, but it was cheap and close to his grandad.

A semi-inflated balloon moved precariously in the first-floor window of his flat. It was a miserable-looking building with a newsagent and opticians on the ground floor. The cladding on the building screamed 1970s. The thought that it was only a temporary arrangement made the situation a little more bearable. He opened his front door, and the resulting draft drew the barely inflated balloon towards him. The huge lettering, 'BIG 40,' barely visible on the crumpled foil, was an immediate reminder that he was now middle-aged. *How am I forty?*

Horace nuzzled into Jack's leg intently, giving Jack a clear indication that food was needed. Jack used his foot to gently usher the cat to one side, but it was useless and Horace stuck to him like a limpet.

"Okay, furball, I take the hint. At least *you* love me, don't you?" said Jack, as he struck the pathetic-looking balloon.

Jack didn't like cats, generally. As a boy, he'd always had a dog and didn't really see the point in cats. They didn't do much other than sleep or eat, it seemed, other than, at their whim, occasionally scratch the shit out of any possession you might have held dear. Horace, then, a timid four-year-old tabby, was an unexpected present addition in his life. Unexpected, as he hadn't expected Helen to leave Horace behind when she'd buggered off. Jack had tried to pluck up the courage to tell the poor creature that the heartless bitch had left, but he didn't have it in him. She'd left them *both*, after all. And in an irrational way, Jack took comfort that

Horace was in the same boat as he was. Misery, as they say, loves company, he supposed.

Helen had left Jack with three things:

1) The lease on a decrepit flat that fortunately only had a couple of months to run
2) The lease on a failing coffee shop, and one that had 'always been her dream'
3) Horace

He did consider a broken heart being the fourth, but sufficient time had now passed for Jack to realise what a bitch she actually was. He was at the stage now where he wanted to get drunk and have casual sex with great-looking women. The problem with that, though, was that he couldn't be bothered going out. So, mostly, he just got drunk at home. Alone, apart from Horace, that is.

The smell of the horrific air freshener was not relenting, so he stripped off in the living room. As he walked towards the kitchen, he caught a glimpse of his chest in the large oak mirror which sat above the faded wooden fireplace. He stopped and had to do a double-take. Slowly, he climbed on the sofa which gave him full visibility of his body. He looked at himself in his underwear and shook his head in disgust. He didn't have a mirror in his room and was struggling to believe what he was looking at.

"I've got a bloody pair of tits!" he shouted.

Horace was unmoved by this revelation, and let out a meow as another reminder that he was quite ready for his tea, thank you.

Jack climbed down from the sofa and moved closer to the mirror. He stood on his toes, and as he struggled to gain his balance, he took his two hands and cupped his cleavage like an expectant teenage girl.

"Horace… what the actual hell are they? I've got boobs. Shittin' hell… I've got man boobs!"

5

He stared intently, but the realisation of what he could see wouldn't go away. His jet-black hair was now a haphazard mix of grey, white, and black, with black now being in the minority. His receding hairline was starting to move towards the egg-shaped bald patch at the back of his head like a reunion of old friends. Laughter lines on his face had moved en masse to form a coalition with the furrows on his forehead. To add to his revulsion, he would now have to go and buy himself a training bra. The flaccid balloon had become a visual representation of his youth, which appeared to be fading before his eyes. His hair was retreating almost as fast as his BMI was escalating. He sat on his tired-looking white leather sofa and reflected. He removed his glasses in a fruitless attempt to make the obvious less visible. The seating position amplified the rolls of fat. He grabbed a handful between his thumb and index finger and started to jiggle it. As his stomach wobbled rhythmically, he gave a look of contempt at the pizza box sat on his glass coffee table. It was empty, apart from a perfectly symmetrical, transparent layer of grease. He extended his foot in a feeble attempt to launch the pizza box but caught his toe on the corner of the table. He yelped in pain and the resulting feminine scream made Horace bolt towards the kitchen. Jack knew it wasn't the pizza's fault and he immediately felt remorse for lashing out at a trusted companion. He pressed his hands into his forehead and released a frustrated groan. "Aww… I've let myself go!"

Emma Reid was small — no taller than 5-foot-2 — but could carry her own body weight in milk. It was a little after 8 a.m. as she took the familiar walk from the Co-Op, laden with large plastic bottles and fruit. The street was desolate apart from the ensemble of pigeons which were a constant frustration for the local retailers. She supported several bottles on her knee as she fumbled for her keys, which, as usual, were located in the darkest recess of her handbag. A tall black wooden shutter protected the internal tiled corridor which they shared with the nail salon on the right-hand side. Before their introduction, the small area provided a convenient toilet facility to passing drunks and as she was always first into work, the cleansing operation would be left to her. The black paint on the internal wooden doors had started to flake, and whilst it was locked, a firm shoulder would open it. The coffee shop looked tired; it needed a makeover. The bright, vibrant decor of the nail salon was a stark contrast to the dark, lacklustre decor of their unit. Minor issues were starting to become a source of irritation. In isolation, they could be forgiven, but they were everywhere — flaking paint, light fittings that no longer worked, torn leather seats. The shop was 'Java the Hut' but the 'J' had long since disappeared. The shop name made no sense. She'd aired her frustrations to Jack, but it was getting worse. Despite the flaws, she loved the place. She knew the name of virtually every customer, what their order would be and what time they'd come in. She'd received a civic award from the Mayor of Douglas because she called on an elderly customer who didn't come in for his morning coffee and paper. He'd fallen — breaking his ankle — and without her compassion, he could have been sat at the foot of his stairs for hours.

The door cautiously opened as an elderly, silver-haired man — stooped over an oak stick — shuffled through. Emma didn't look. She didn't need to. It was 8:20 a.m. sharp, and she knew what that meant. "Morning, Derek. Take a seat, my lovely, I'll bring your tea over!"

Derek didn't really speak much, but his face instantly lit up when he saw Emma. The shop wasn't huge, two tables wide, and long — narrowing towards the counter and stairs at the rear. The two front windows were vast and flooded the shop with natural light. They were the perfect porthole into the world that passed by the shop. Derek took his usual seat on the right-hand side, with his back to the wall, giving him a clear view up the main street. They were just off the main shopping area but still on a main thoroughfare. The business district was on their doorstep, as were an ever-increasing number of upmarket apartments, eager to take advantage of the nearby marina. Despite assurance from Emma, he always came in early as he felt he was imposing by taking a full table just to have his mug of black tea with one sugar.

She soon appeared with his usual mug and a radiant smile, smartly dressed in her black skirt and shirt — covered by a dark green apron with a picture of Jabba the Hutt drinking a large, steaming cup of coffee. On first appearance, she could pass for Mediterranean, with her olive skin and dark eyes. Her jet-black hair was tied back where her pencil was carefully placed, poised to take an order. "Here you go, Derek. Be careful, it's hot," she cautioned. "Also, I made this for you. Happy birthday, Derek!" she said, handing him a little something extra. "You can share it with those beautiful grandchildren of yours," she added cheerfully.

He opened the white cardboard box to reveal a lavish chocolate cake, decorated with generous layers of icing, and with a single white candle sat in the middle. He closed the box over and reached out, taking one of Emma's hands, which he held tenderly. "Thank you, Emma. Thank you very much," he said softly.

A steady stream of customers moved through the shop, but there was no sign of Jack. *Where is that lazy sod?* she wondered. But her warm welcome to her customers was unwavering as she handled the machinery like a master, easily containing the morning rush, which, to be fair, was not as busy as it once was. As she cleared the tables nearest to the window, she became aware of a figure moving through the street, drawing near. She avoided eye contact, assuming it to be a drunk on the way to one of the two less salubrious local watering holes which opened early. The silhouette moved from her peripheral vision and hunched directly in front of her. She was startled and began to panic as there was no one else in the shop. The man on the other side of the glass placed both hands on the large windowpane, as if supporting himself, and his chin was tucked into his chest so she could not see his face. He was dressed in tight, dishevelled denim shorts that sat just above his knee and a t-shirt that clung to him like it had shrunk in the wash. She moved slowly backward, towards the rear of the shop, as the man lumbered towards the entrance. For a fleeting moment the thought of locking the door seemed sensible, but she knew those doors would have no defence against a strong gust of wind let alone a determined drunk. He let out a pained whimper as he moved through the door and fell to his knees.

"I know karate!" yelled Emma, in a firm, assured tone.

She decided to go on the offensive and flailed her arms behind her back whilst maintaining eye contact. She was frantically trying to grab a possible projectile, and gratefully retrieved a curved object that she then launched in the direction of the man — who was still kneeling, but with his head now buried in the oak laminate flooring.

"Get out!" she shouted, as she began to throw the items she'd fumbled for. In the blink of an eye, several large potatoes tore through the air with precision. One of them caught him perfectly on the side of the right temple. He sank to the floor like a fallen tree, barely managing to roll over onto his back. He instinctively reached for his throbbing head as Emma ran towards him to release another volley.

"Aww, shit!" he said, trying to move into a seated position. Emma was directly above him and placed a foot firmly on his chest, preventing his progress.

"Emma, stop! For the love of God, please stop... It's me, Jack!"

Emma didn't remove her foot until Jack moved his hands and she could confirm who it was. It was Jack, and for a moment she increased the pressure on his chest.

"Jack, you complete tool. Are you trying to kill me?"

She removed her foot and extended her hand to help him to his feet. The potato had split on impact and a dribble of juice ran down his right cheek. Jack was now on his feet and covered in sweat. The brown figure-hugging t-shirt was emblazoned with the face of SpongeBob SquarePants and sported an impressive damp patch on the rear.

He was struggling for breath and reached for a bottle of water in the chiller cabinet, taking several appreciative slugs.

"Why are you dressed like that, Jack? You look like someone that should be on a register," said Emma, as she began to clean up the remnants of the potato.

"I ran to work!" replied Jack. "Well... when I say ran, I mean walked. Mostly walked."

"If you walked, why do you look like that, a sweating mess?"

"I started off running, until I couldn't breathe... which was about three hundred metres. Then I walked along the seafront until I saw a couple of girls I went to school with who were running. I didn't want to look stupid, so I started running the last half mile."

"You didn't want to look stupid? You do realise what you're wearing? Those shorts look like something from an eighties' workout video, and do you think that t-shirt could be any tighter? And since when did you start running?"

Jack's breathing had returned to normal as he collapsed into a chair. "I think I've put a bit of weight on, Emma. I'm supporting a little extra timber!"

Emma didn't seem at all surprised by this revelation. "I'd say it's more than a little, Jack."

"What, you noticed? Why didn't you say anything?" he said, with a pained expression.

"Jack, it's pretty obvious. But, do a bit of running and you'll get rid of it in no time."

"You're an old friend, Emma. You could have told me. I'd have told you if you'd put a few pounds on."

"No you wouldn't!" scoffed Emma. "Remember, you let me walk around here for an hour with my skirt tucked into my knickers!"

"The old boys loved it, that's why! Besides, I told you about your moustache!" replied Jack.

"Wait... what? What moustache? You didn't tell me about any moustache. I haven't got a moustache!" she insisted.

Jack paused for a moment. "Well... I thought I did. Besides, it wasn't me that noticed. It was Postman Pete."

"You and bloody Pete have been talking about me having a moustache?"

"No! Well, not at first. It was your hairy forearms that got us onto the subject."

Emma stomped towards the nearest mirror. "No wonder we've never got any customers. They're probably afraid that you'll eat them, or Chewbacca here will moult into their soup!"

The sound of sirens echoed through the street and Emma panicked that someone had witnessed her assault on Jack and called the police. She was relieved as an ambulance pulled up outside the locksmiths, further up the street. She moved to the front of the shop, under the guise of cleaning the tables.

"You nosey old trout!" shouted Jack from his seated position. "What's going on?"

"One of them has gone in the shop and the other is talking to Postman Pete," she replied, with her face all but pressed to the glass. "Shit... they've seen me!" said Emma, leaving a perfect imprint of her cheek as she withdrew.

Pete frowned at Emma as he walked in. "Caught you rubbernecking!"

"I was showing concern, that's all!" she protested.

Pete had a deliberately stern look on his face, but Emma wasn't biting. She ignored him which had an instant effect, as he shuffled impatiently, expecting a reaction. Pete was arguably the biggest drama queen in Douglas and Emma was convinced he fancied Jack. He was openly gay, and possibly the campest mailman in the entire postal service. He was an icon, one of those characters that you either knew or knew someone who knew him. He'd previously worked in the holiday camps, a theatrical type who would often 'tread the boards' — he was exceptionally busy when they were looking for the pantomime dame type cast. Nothing happened in the Isle of Man without Pete knowing about it, and his job as a postman was a perfect pretext to force an invite into people's lives on a daily basis. Emma liked him; he was a 'bitch' of the highest order and his gossip was always of the finest calibre. She was slightly annoyed, however. If Pete had noticed her moustache, it would have now been relayed to the entire street.

"Well… what's going on?" asked Emma, reluctantly.

"Ray's had a funny turn again. He's been in the shop all night."

"Shit," said Jack. "I saw him, just, sat there. I thought he was just drunk again. Poor sod."

Ray's family had run the locksmiths for generations. It was once a thriving business. Sadly, Ray had a penchant for red wine, spending most of his days in a drunken stupor. Jack would often look in on him, but in truth he was beyond hope. He was in his late sixties, well over twenty stone, and his liver must have been like a walnut.

Pete pulled a handful of envelopes out of his delivery bag — neatly encased in an elastic band — and handed them to Jack. Pete and Jack shared a knowing glance as the obvious red ink shone like a beacon through paper windows.

"Are you going to open them, Jack?" asked Emma.

Jack said nothing.

"Oh, give them here!" said Emma, ripping open the envelopes.

She looked at the letters, back towards Jack, and then onto the letters again. It was like a parent opening their child's exam results. Jack hadn't opened his post for weeks. The irony of scolding his grandfather for doing the exact same thing was not lost on him.

He looked sheepish, hoping Emma would soften the blow.

"Jaaack," she said, in a drawn-out, forceful voice. "This isn't pretty. We're overdue on the rent, rates, and insurance. The good news, though, is that your gym membership is only going up by two pounds a month this year."

Even Pete — the queen of gossip — was rueful. He loved Jack and Emma, and coming into the shop was a feature of his day. He'd be lost if the shop closed down.

"Aww," groaned Jack. "I tried, but this place is dead. It's those corporate shysters that keep opening up, they're taking all the business." He stared vacantly for a moment. "Hang on, what gym membership? I didn't even know I was a member of a gym."

"You could have fooled me!" remarked Emma. "We need to come up with something and quick, Jack!"

He sank his head in his hands. Pete took the opportunity to sit on the arm of his chair and place a friendly arm around his shoulder.

"Jack…" said Pete. "Those shorts are a little… neat. Are they not?"

Emma smiled, unsure if Pete was criticising or approving.

"On a positive note," said Pete, jumping to his feet in his overly animated manner. "It looks like you've got new neighbours!"

"Let me guess," said Jack. "Another coffee shop, to add to the seventeen already in town?"

"I don't know," replied Pete. "The windows are fogged out, but the lights are on and I could see people inside. It's good for the street though, Jack. Another shop will bring more punters down this side of town."

Emma scurried outside, followed closely by Pete. They fabricated a conversation as Emma gaped over his shoulder, searching for a clue. There was no sign of life, but she was delighted to see the lights on, in the unit that had been desolate for months.

Jack appeared a moment later, and made no effort to disguise his intentions. He walked straight over to the window and strained to see through the smeared glass, but it was useless. The missing sign above their shop now appeared more apparent with the unit next door illuminated.

"We need to get this place fixed up," said Jack. "If this place goes tits-up, who's going to employ us?"

"Speak for yourself!" said Emma. "Besides, we'll be fine. We just need to come up with a plan to get some new customers in!"

She linked arms with Jack and burrowed her head into his shoulder. "Jack… you really need to go for a shower, you stink. Why don't you go and use the ones in the gym that you're paying for and never used!"

Jack laughed, forcing her head closer to his armpit. "Cheeky! Your skirt is tucked into your knickers, again! Oh, and Thomas Magnum called. He wants his moustache back!"

Chapter Two

It was a little after six a.m. and already humid. Jack stood
with his back against the sandstone-coloured wall of a
large multi-storey car park. Sweat formed on his forehead
despite his lack of movement. He felt a wave of apprehension
as his foot started to tap in time to the dull beat radiating
from the building opposite. A steady stream of people made
their way energetically through the inconspicuous glass
doors. His denim shorts were, by now, a distant memory.
Much to Emma's relief, they were currently to be found
under the shop sink absorbing drops of water caused by an
ageing washer.

His blue Slazenger t-shirt was a little more forgiving and
his grey Adidas shorts were significantly more complimentary
than his previous efforts. The blue suede Adidas Samba
trainers, a throwback to his youth, were immaculate on
their first outing. He smiled as he thought of being back at
high school. A new pair of trainers was an invitation for
every halfwit to stamp their mark onto your new purchase,
white trainers being the principal target. He took one final
look in his rucksack, taking a mental inventory: boxer
shorts — check; shorts and shirt for work — check; deodorant
— check; towel — check; socks — *bugger!*

A brief lull in the passing flow of people was his
opportunity. He puffed out his cheeks and made his way up
the narrow staircase — three flights in total. The heat inside

was amplified, and with the effort from the steps, the sweat fell freely down his cheeks. He approached the large wooden desk and was greeted by a brute of a lad whose biceps were bigger than Jack's legs.

He greeted Jack with a jolly smile. "You're keen!" he said, acknowledging the pink cheeks and wet face. "Early morning run?"

Jack nodded his head in agreement. "Best way to start the day," he replied, wiping the sweat which had now reached his neck.

"It's been a little while since I last came," said Jack, sheepishly. "I couldn't seem to find my card."

"Ah, no problem, I thought I didn't recognise the face. What's the name?"

"Jack Tate."

The young Hercules stared intently at his screen. "I've got no Jack Tate listed. When were you last here?"

"Three months, maybe?" replied Jack, lying.

He took Jack's details and deferred to his manual records in the office. Jack walked to the window to the left of the desk where a spin class was in full throw. A variety of body shapes of various ages sweated vigorously to the backdrop of neon lights, as a small, dark-haired lady shouted encouragement.

Several minutes elapsed and Jack was starting to get impatient.

"Sorry, Jack, but I can't find a record for you?" he said, raising his hands in submission.

Jack was hot and getting frustrated. "I've been paying you thirty-seven pound, ninety-nine pence a month, for the last two years."

Hercules could sense the frustration in the voice and seemed to instinctively increase his body mass like an agitated pufferfish. This didn't go unnoticed by Jack, who took a more conciliatory approach. He reached for his mobile phone, opening his online banking application. He nodded his head slowly as the page loaded. "Ah, there… that's it — thirty-seven pound, ninety-nine, Fitness Works."

The young lad smiled and leaned back into his chair, placing both his hands on top of his head. Without speaking, he pointed a finger slowly towards the sign above his head.

Jack put his phone away as his cheeks flushed. "This isn't Fitness Works, is it? I should probably just go."

Feeling slightly dejected, the thought of staying fat was appealing. He'd made such a palaver about his 'gym debut' that Emma would destroy him if he gave up at the first hurdle. He pushed on and was soon on an exercise bike, in the correct gym, armed with a new membership card. It wasn't the traditional bike but the one where you're seated, with a backrest. The position you'd be in riding a pedal go-kart. His initial trepidation was eased as he reached the two-mile mark with relative ease. With contempt, he raised the level from one to fourteen, and the increased resistance was immediate. *No pain, no gain, C'mon Jack.*

He gripped the metal strip on the side handlebars and his heart rate flashed onto the screen: 162. It didn't mean anything to him. He knew a heart rate of zero wasn't a sign of optimum health, but other than that, he was clueless. The sleeves on his t-shirt were used to wipe his brow and were now sodden. Sweat appeared sporadically on his stomach and chest, gushing from his forehead. His glasses started to slide down his nose like driftwood on a violent river, so he removed them and placed them into the vacant cup holder. A combination of being short-sighted and sweat in his eyes rendered him all but blind as he stared vacantly. He could see the miles increasing at a very leisurely rate, but the rest was a blur. Unfortunately, in the area Jack had focussed his attention were two exceptionally attractive ladies completing floor exercises. One of them pointed the gawping Jack out to the other, but his gaze was unwavering. As they stood in their tight Lycra outfits, Jack rubbed his sweaty palms on his new Adidas shorts, much to the disgust of the girls, who were now walking towards him at pace.

"You big, dirty, sweaty perv!" shouted one of the girls.

"Loser!" shouted the other.

Jack was oblivious, and a little unsure where the venom was directed. He gave a contrite smile, but this was more out of sympathy than an admission of guilt.

The five-mile mark appeared majestically on the screen. Jack felt like Sir Edmund Hillary ascending Everest. As he stopped pedalling, he felt like a pioneer; he wouldn't be surprised if the entire gym applauded in unison. He dried his face and replaced his glasses, but the gym was all but empty, apart from two women, talking to a male member of staff and pointing in his general direction. His euphoria was soon replaced with a stomach cramp. Unfortunately, the exercise and scrambled eggs were not good bedfellows, causing him to make a hasty retreat to the changing rooms, and he was that damp that he thought it may already have been too late.

There were only two stalls and one was taken. He wrestled the cord on his shorts — neatly tied in a double knot — with increasing anxiety. Sweat continued to run down his face which further hampered his vision. A wave of abject fear ran through him as the pains in his stomach intensified. He tried to pull his shorts in desperation, but every time he interfered with the knot, it tightened further. Jack threw the changing room door open and moved as fast as he could towards the reception desk. He walked in a strangely rhythmic manner as he clenched his buttocks in an attempt to delay the inevitable.

"Scissors," said Jack. "Please, I need to borrow your scissors."

The greying, mature receptionist smiled as she took her glasses from her head and sluggishly looked through the knee-high filing cabinet behind her. Jack shuffled with increasing intensity as he began to comprehend the reality of what may happen at any moment. She engaged Jack in small talk, but her words were lost on him. He leaned over the countertop and saw the scissors sat next to the computer monitor. He reached out with such velocity that the receptionist recoiled in fear. He attacked the waistband of his shorts in a series of stabbing motions. The fabric initially resisted, but with a bit of coaxing the shorts soon slackened. Such was the indiscriminate assault that Jack hadn't notice the sharp blade had continued through the fabric. He slapped the scissors back on the desk and turned vigorously towards the changing rooms. As he moved, the remaining shards of fabric burst free, and the shorts fell towards his ankles, causing him to stumble. He fell to his knees initially, but the momentum forced him further forward, laying like he was praying at Mecca. Much to the visible disgust of the receptionist who was now stood looking at Jack from a rear perspective, it was apparent there had been a small seepage. The two girls who'd vented their anger at Jack had also appeared on their way back to the dressing room and looked down on Jack with repulsion. His ankles were locked together, so he used his arms to crawl towards the bathroom whilst trying to contain the fragile state of his underpants.

He sat in the cubicle and the sense of relief was immediate. His joy was temporary as he reached for the toilet paper. There are only a few scenarios in life that can replicate the feeling of desperation when you realise there is no toilet paper. Among these are:

1) Smashing your mobile phone
2) Losing your wallet
3) Unable to find your keys at 2 a.m.

His kit bag was sat on the bench in the dressing room. He knew his options were restricted. His underpants had already completed the ultimate sacrifice. His shorts were non-existent. His t-shirt wouldn't flush. Jack took off one of his socks and smiled at the current situation.

Showered, dressed and wearing one sock, Jack picked up his bag and made a hasty exit. Fortunately, the reception desk was empty — he reasoned they were checking CCTV for an imminent police investigation. His gym debut nearly faltered, but despite the degrading start to the day, he was proud of himself. It was an emotion that was alien to him, as it had been a long time since he'd felt pride in himself. His step quickened as he walked through the main shopping street. He threw a nonchalant glance at his reflection in the glass windows of a ladies clothes shop. He'd only cycled a few short miles, but his stomach felt and looked tighter. Even the exhausted-looking signage at the front of his shop wouldn't dampen his mood. He used his thumbnail to remove several obvious areas of flaking paint which only served to highlight, how much the shop was in need of decoration. There were several greying lumps attached to the wooden framework of the shop front. Only after he'd removed one did he realise they were discarded chewing gum. It stuck like a limpet clinging to a rock, and try as he might, the remaining pieces resisted his efforts. Undeterred, Jack placed his gym bag on the ground and removed his left trainer and used the heel as an improvised chisel. As the last bit conceded, Jack became aware of a wonderful scent of perfume that caused him to take a deep, second lungful.

"That's an unusual way to clean your windows!" said a gentle voice behind him.

It sounded like Emma, so Jack continued to remove errant flakes of paint.

"So much for the gym!" said Jack. "I've just shit myself and had to wipe my ass on a sock! I think I'm also going to have a restraining order taken out on me."

There was no response, so Jack arched his neck. "You're not Emma?"

"No… I'm not. But, when I see her, I'll be sure to tell her about the sock."

He blushed as he turned. "I'm Jack. I own this fine establishment." He went to shake her hand, but as he did, several lumps of chewing gum fell from his grasp. The girl took a step back, smiling awkwardly.

He became very aware that he was stood with one bare foot, holding his trainer in his left hand. "This looks a bit odd," he said. "I don't usually stand in the street with one shoe on, but my sock was…"

"Yes, I got that… at the gym."

"I'm not, you know, crazy or anything. I've just joined the gym and I had scrambled eggs. Don't do that by the way, or if you do, make sure they have toilet roll."

"Can I just start this conversation again?" asked Jack.

"Yes! Yes, we should!" was the immediate response.

"Well, you know me! And judging by the coffee cup you're holding, you've also met Emma who I work with?"

"Yes. Good coffee by the way! I'm Hayley, Hayley Scott. I'm your new neighbour."

She was lovely, and Jack was struggling to string a sentence together as he stared into her huge blue eyes.

"Great! So you've got the shop next door. What do you do?"

Hayley pointed proudly to the vibrant red rose on her immaculate white blouse and then to the sign above the newly painted shop front. "I'm a florist."

"*The Enchanted Florist.* That's a great name!" said Jack.

The sign was commanding, with gold lettering on a white background. A yellow rose formed the 'I' in the word florist.

"Anyway… I should really get on. Busy day!" said Hayley, with a feigned enthusiasm.

"Of course," replied Jack. "We're captains of industry." Jack half closed his eyes and he could hear the inner voice, *will you just shut up, you fool.*

Jack shuffled into the shop and collapsed into a chair nearest to the door.

"You met Hayley?" shouted Emma.

"Yep!" conceded Jack.

"You made a tit out of yourself, didn't you?"

"I did, yes. A full-on forty-four DD-sized tit. The kind of tit you see that hangs down by your belt. I don't get it, I used to be okay with the women."

"It can't have been that bad, you were only talking to her for a couple of minutes."

He sunk his head further into his hands and groaned. "I threw fossilised chewing gum, and I told her I'd just shit myself. As far as introductions go, it probably wasn't the best."

"Memorable, though?" laughed Emma. "She was certainly pretty."

"She was lovely," sighed Jack. "She's a florist."

"Your mum phoned for you. You need to call her back. She sounded pissed off with you."

He paused for a moment and as he hadn't spoken to her for a week, he mused how he could possibly have irritated her.

Emma could see the vacant expression. "Something about your grandad being arrested."

"What! You're joking, right? Tell me you're joking."

"I'm just telling you what she said. Oh, she said something about Randy Sandy, and then screamed something about *why didn't you stop him.*"

"Oh, shit!" said Jack, who was now pacing back and forth.

"Who is Sandy?" asked Emma.

"She's the local bike. Generous with her affections, for the right price."

"She's a prostitute?"

"She was… but there are not many willing to pay, these days."

"You let your grandad go with a prostitute? No wonder your mum is pissed with you."

"He was in the army, he's not bloody stupid. I better go and get Grandad out of jail — and there's a sentence I didn't think I'd ever utter. Are you okay here?"

"I think we'll be okay," replied Emma, gesturing to the empty seats. "And stay away from Sandy!"

Jack pushed the Vespa onto its centre stand and removed his helmet. He caught sight of his mother and raised a hand in acknowledgement. She was petite but well-built, and her white dental nurse uniform made her look like an evil assistant in an early Bond film.

"Your bloody grandad has been arrested," she said, marching purposefully towards him. "We'll never live this down!" she continued, covering her face with her hands. "Why did you not stop him?"

She continued with her tirade, and although it was serious, Jack couldn't help but smile at the situation.

"What are you bloody smiling at?" she said, through pursed lips, shouting, but at the same time, trying to whisper. Jack loved his mother and knew exactly what buttons to push to wind her up. Smiling when she was angry was one of them.

"He's *your* father, so how is this possibly *my* fault?" protested Jack.

"You're thick as thieves, you two. You must have known what he was doing. The mucky old sod!"

Jack walked away. It wasn't that he was ignoring her, but he couldn't stifle his smile and was concerned his mum was about to erupt. He walked into the reception area and was greeted by a surly female receptionist sat behind a security screen. She didn't speak, but pressed a button on her side of the screen which made a concealed speaker start to crackle.

"I'm here to see my grandad. I believe you may be holding him."

"What name?"

"Geoffrey Smith," whispered Jack.

She skimmed through the papers on her desk and paused. "Eighty years old! That's got to be a record," she said, with a wry smile.

"Yes, we're all very proud of him," replied Jack.

"I'll phone the arresting officer for you. Take a seat, over there."

"Oh," she said, pushing herself closer towards the screen. "Is that, her?" she said, looking Jack's mother up and down.

"Who?" asked Jack.

She looked back at her notes for a moment. "Her in the nurse's outfit. Is that Sandy?"

Jack turned and shook his head for a moment. "Yes!" he whispered. "That's her, apparently. It's medical day today."

Jack's mother was smiling nervously as the receptionist gave her a look of contempt and pointed her out to a colleague.

A steady stream of people passed through the reception area. There were the remorseful, perhaps too much to drink the night before, and the aggressive arrogant type, who didn't appear fazed. There were those emaciated by years of substance abuse. The atmosphere was intimidating, and Jack could understand the receptionist being aloof. It would take a resolute personality to make sense of the chaos that would unfurl each day. Jack became more solemn as he thought of his grandad locked up.

A cheery-looking policeman appeared from behind the reception desk. "You're here for Geoffrey?" he said to Jack. "Please, come with me."

Jack's mum was outside having a cigarette, and in the circumstances, he felt it was best dealt with 'man-to-man.' He was led to a small room where he was relieved to see his grandad, sitting, holding a cup of tea. He looked dejected. "You okay, Grandad?"

"He's been telling us about his army career," said the constable. "Your grandad is a real character."

"Is he in any trouble?" asked Jack.

"No, he should be okay. It's up to my gaffer, but I think a friendly warning is all that's required. To be honest, he was in the wrong place at the wrong time. We've had a few complaints from neighbours, and it was only his bad luck he was there when we called 'round. We had to be seen to be doing something. Your grandad told us that he only bought her some shopping and that nothing had happened. The lady confirmed this as well."

"Can I take him home?"

"Yes. I'll *escort* — excuse the pun — you out. We'll be in touch if there is any further action, but it should be fine. Geoffrey, it's been a real pleasure to meet you."

Geoffrey nodded and walked into the corridor. As Jack went to follow, the officer placed a hand on his shoulder: "You need to keep an eye on your grandad. He's a lovely old boy, but he's lonely. This Sandy one has been keeping him company, but the next one could take more than a few days' worth of shopping off him. He was in tears before and I tried to tell him it would be okay. I think he is just a bit ashamed as well. If you need anything or think anyone is taking advantage of him, give me a call."

Jack was grateful, and shook the policeman's hand and then walked his grandad through to the main reception area. Jack's mother was furious, but could see the ashen expression on her father's face. Rather than issuing a reprimand, she warmly embraced him. "You silly old bugger," she said softly. "Let's get you home."

"Lunch must have been busy?" asked Jack, admiring the banknotes in the usually sparse-looking till. "Sorry to leave you on your own."

"It's fine. Did the vice squad lock him up?" asked Emma.

Jack shook his head. "No, just a verbal warning with no further action. He looked really sad Emma. I've never seen him like that. The policeman said he was in tears. I know he misses Gran, but I don't think we appreciated just how much."

"They were together for a long time, Jack."

"I know, but you just assume that time is a great healer, 'stiff upper lip' and all that."

Emma moved closer and put a gentle hand on his shoulder. "Maybe he's just really lonely and Sandy would listen to him — albeit for a price."

"That's what the policeman said. He needs to make some friends, but it must be difficult at that age."

"We should do something in here, Jack, a social club for the elderly. It'd help the older people and bring new customers in."

Jack looked underwhelmed. "I don't want them in here, stinking of piss. They'd put the regulars off."

"What regulars?" laughed Emma. "The only regulars we have are the older ones."

"We get the office trade as well!"

"No, Jack, you said it yourself, most of the younger crowd go to the branded shops — *corporate shysters,* wasn't it?"

"Maybe, but the 'blue-rinse brigade' nursing a cup of tea for three hours isn't going to fill the till!"

The impromptu business development meeting was interrupted by a gentle knock on the door. Jack responded by sucking his stomach in and arching his back. "Hayley!" he said enthusiastically. "Great to see you again, what can I get you?"

"Hi guys, sorry to bother you, but do you know what day the bin men come?"

"Tuesday," said Jack. "Usually about seven a.m."

"Thanks. The coffee was great, by the way." Hayley presented Emma with a vibrant bunch of red roses displayed in an opaque crystal vase. "These are for you. Well, for the shop, I mean. I could do with the vase back when you're done?"

"They're beautiful," said Emma, placing them on a shelf near to the counter. "It should be *us* buying *you* flowers to welcome you to the neighbourhood."

"You're welcome. And sorry to interrupt you both."

"You're not interrupting," said Emma. "We're just wondering how to get people through the door. Short of dragging them in! We were thinking about a social, possibly dating club, for the elderly."

"That's a wonderful idea, guys, it really is. My grandmother would love to come. She's a real chatterbox, you'd never get rid of her. Not enough people do things for the elderly and I think it'd be a huge success. You'd be welcome to put a poster up in my shop, if you like?"

"That's right," said Jack confidently. "I was just saying to Emma, in fact, that we needed to put something back into the community, help the vulnerable and the frail."

Emma was about to twist the knife, but she figured he deserved a break and judging by the vain trembling in his neck, he clearly liked Hayley.

"That's really sweet, Jack. I'd be happy to help out as well," replied Hayley.

"Oh, he's a real pillar of the community. Once you get over the daft persona, he's actually not too bad," said Emma.

Jack's stomach expanded to normal size as the door closed. "Thanks, Emma, I owe you. Aww, but I'm going to have to do something about it now."

"What's the worst that can happen, Jack? We get a few more customers through the door and it's not going to cost you any money to do. Besides, it will make Hayley think you're… well, less of a tool."

Emma stood in the middle of the floor and slowly looked around. "Let's do this, Jack. We're going to set up the Island's first social and dating club for the elderly."

"Dating as well? I'll need to stock up on the blue pills. What are we going to call this club?"

She paused for a moment. "We, Jack, we are going to open *The Lonely Heart Club*."

Jack was unimpressed. "For the crowd you're looking at, you should call it The Lonely Heart Attack Club!"

Emma smiled, for which she was immediately guilty. "This, Jack, is going to bring customers into your business and keep me in a job that I'm still not actually sure I want."

"Come here," said Jack, taking Emma in a friendly embrace. "It's a wonderful idea and a wonderful name. You're the best friend and employee I could ever wish for. Also, if this gets me laid with Hayley, then even better."

Chapter Three

It was early and the phone had already rung incessantly for over an hour. The answering machine had reached its capacity, and emitted a piercing tone that reverberated throughout the small two-bedroomed flat. Cellophane-wrapped brochures and envelopes emblazoned with bright red lettering all but covered the carpet in the entrance hall and extended further into the living area. A large wooden oak sideboard was almost obscured by pile after pile of unopened correspondence and the drawers spilt the excess onto the carpet. A small white cocker spaniel barely lifted his head as the morning post increased the escalating pile further.

Derek would normally be dressed by this time, but today had been an effort and he sat in his grey flannel pyjamas. He loved to sit in his cream leather reclining chair and look at the distant marina on one side and the sprawling Isle of Man hills on the other. He'd been in the flat for sixty-five years and he often joked with his neighbour, Anne, that he was still looking for something bigger to move into. The flat was near the town centre and a short walk to the shops and his local pub where he would venture for two pints of bitter on a Friday night. He eased his feet into his blue slippers and glanced with trepidation in the direction of the front door. He pushed himself from the chair and pulled a biscuit from his pocket, which he held in his left hand. Charlie immediately leapt up, and gratefully accepted the treat. "Good boy, Charlie," he said affectionately. He carefully shuffled to the door, taking care to avoid the sporadic envelopes which were slippery if stood on. As he moved through the hall, making his way to the door, he gave a frustrated groan as he straightened a fallen photo frame which had succumbed to the mound of paper; he smiled at the picture of his beloved Helen. He held onto the table in the vestibule to steady himself and stooped to collect the discarded post. Without review, he brought them into the kitchen and placed them onto a further increasing pile. The white box containing the sumptuous chocolate cake with one candle sat on the kitchen table, minus one small piece, which he'd indulged in the previous evening. How he longed to share the cake with his two grandchildren. However, his cherished memories were soon interrupted by the phone.

The flat was immaculate apart from the mail. He put his breakfast dishes carefully back in the oak welsh dresser and neatly folded the tea towel. He moved the cake so that the tabletop was now empty, and took a seat. He reached for the white envelope in his pocket and as he removed it, several more biscuits fell to the floor, gratefully received by Charlie. He placed it in the centre of the table and glanced at the clock. It didn't feel correct to not be dressed at this time. He closed the door on Charlie and left him in the kitchen, as he often did during his visits to the shop. He carefully took the small ladders that were only three rungs tall, but sufficient to allow him access to remove the hatch to the loft. To avoid slipping, he ascended barefoot. He took a narrow pole with a hook in the end and pulled down the loft hatch, revealing a set of extendable ladders and a further hoard of discarded letters. He'd installed a handrail inside the loft hatch to aide access, but it'd been a long time since he had the mobility to fully access the space. Now, it was simply used as an overflow.

Derek took the cord from his dressing gown and placed it neatly through the handrail, so that it formed a loop. He was a master of knots from his time in the merchant navy, and he'd soon formed a perfect circle which felt strong enough to carry his weight. He took the bottom of the circle and twisted it once. He looked at the picture of Helen on the hall table, and took the newly created, smaller loop and placed it around his neck. He could hear Charlie bark in the kitchen as he shuffled towards the end of the steps, which he began to rock slowly back and forth. He thought of happier times and had a wry smile as the letterbox opened once again. He thought his final sight would be the thing that had driven him to his current position.

"Derek. Derek, luv, are you there? I've been knocking but there was no answer. Derek, it's Emma from the coffee shop."

Derek was startled, and instantly stood upright in order to relieve any pressure on his neck, throwing the cord out of sight into the recess of the loft.

"Derek. Derek, can you hear me? I missed you this morning. I had your tea ready for you."

He moved towards the door. "Yes... I'm here." He slowly opened the door, taking care to move the visible post from view. He stood in the partially opened door frame, greeted by Emma and her infectious smile.

"Emma, what a lovely unexpected surprise. So nice to see you. You must excuse my attire, I've been rather tardy this morning."

"Aww, thanks, Derek. Please don't think I'm crazy calling, but I always worry if one of my regulars doesn't show up."

"However did you find me?"

"It wasn't hard, Derek. I knew you lived around here so I knocked on a couple of doors and said I was looking for a lovely gentleman called Derek who used to be in the navy. Everyone I spoke to smiled when I mentioned your name. You must have a lot of friends around here! Anyway, I wanted to check on you and make sure you were well and to tell you about our new social club. It is for anyone who wants to come along and make new friends, but probably more directed to the—"

"Old codgers," teased Derek.

"*Mature crowd* is what I'd have gone for," laughed Emma. "Anyway, here is a little brochure with the times. We'd love to see you there and will I see you at the usual time tomorrow?"

"Yes, yes, of course, Emma. I'm sorry if I worried you, and the club sounds like a wonderful idea."

The paper chaos was difficult to ignore, and Emma took a step forward, her tone becoming concerned. "Derek, I don't mean to pry… but, are you okay?"

He paused for a moment and lowered his head, taking several deep breaths as his head rocked slowly. He raised a visibly shaking hand and wiped a solitary tear from his cheek. "They just won't leave me alone, Emma. They mean well, but they just don't give me a moment."

Emma moved closer and took his hand in hers. "Who, Derek?"

His shoulders convulsed as the tears now began to flow freely. "Derek, whatever is the matter? Let's get you inside."

She put her hands around his shoulders and escorted him in. She was overwhelmed by the sheer volume of unopened post; it had all but consumed the flat. Derek had become accustomed to it, but to an outsider it was clear something wasn't right. Emma pulled a chair close to where he was sat and again took his hands. "Derek, do you mind me asking what's going on? This amount of post is not normal."

"I told you, they won't leave me alone, Emma."

Almost as if on cue, the phone rang once again, and rang until intercepted by the answering machine.

"Who is *they?*" asked Emma, who was interrupted by the phone ringing again.

"People looking for money. They just won't stop."

Emma was confused and took a pile of the unopened post, sat near to the fire hearth. "Do you mind if I take a look, Derek?"

She opened an envelope and it contained an innocuous brochure from a children's charity. She looked at Derek for a moment and opened another and another. It was a further request from the same charity but each one contained a further harrowing story designed to pull at the heartstrings. Each pile contained an emotional plea from another charity, but it was unrelenting, each one bordering on begging.

"Derek, you poor thing, how long has this been going on?"

He shrugged his shoulders. "I don't know, eighteen months, perhaps two years? It started when I gave a donation over the phone. I received more phone calls and I tried to help. I tried to help them all. Then the letters started arriving. Just a few at first and again, I helped where I could. Soon there were too many and I couldn't help them all. The phone calls continued but I told them I couldn't help anymore, but they didn't stop. They made me feel cheap and that I should really be trying harder. I tried, Emma, I really tried to help but I ran out of money. They just won't leave me alone."

Emma put her hand over her face. "Derek, you're not cheap. You're a wonderfully generous person who has been bullied into helping, by people who are paid to pester for donations."

She dropped to her knees and moved closer. "Derek, how much have you given them?"

He was bewildered. "I don't know? Everything, I think."

The phone rang again, the third time since she'd arrived, but this time she picked up the handset. She listened intently for a moment before firmly interrupting. "No, he doesn't live here, and please stop calling immediately or I'll report you!"

"You can get help, Derek. We can make all of this go away. Can I speak with your family for you and explain what's happened?"

"They don't live here anymore. My daughter moved to Italy with her husband and the two children three years ago."

"Does she come to see you?" asked Emma.

"No. She's busy in her job and I'd just be a hindrance. She does phone me, sometimes."

"I can help if you'd like me to? I just need to speak with the post office and the phone company. We'll also need to take you to the bank, Derek, make sure they stop the payments and stop any others from going out. Do you think I should phone your daughter? Would that be okay with you?"

"I'd like that very much, Emma. Thank you!"

"Seeing as how you missed your cup of tea this morning, what say I go and put that kettle on for you?"

She smiled and moved towards the kitchen, where she was once again staggered by the post. As the kettle boiled, she began to create piles to take out to the bin. It was difficult to ignore the hand-written note that had been left on the kitchen table, and she froze as she read the shaky writing: "*To whoever finds this letter, I'm truly sorry.*"

She brought the cup of tea through. "Here you go, Derek. I couldn't help but notice this letter in the kitchen. Do I need to be worried about leaving you, Derek? Should I phone social services for you?"

He looked a little embarrassed as he took the letter. He shook his head as he ripped the letter into several pieces. "No, Emma, I promise I'll be fine. You've done more than enough, and besides, I'm looking forward to coming to your social club!"

"Okay, I'll help you sort all of this, Derek, I promise. We're also going to be doing a speed dating night, which will be good fun."

"I'll need to find my good teeth!" he joked.

"Where have you been?" barked Jack. "It's been heaving in here this morning!"

The dishwasher said otherwise, as did the contents of the till which confirmed that Emma hadn't really been missed. "I've been with Derek, I told you I was going to look in on him."

"Which one is Derek?"

"Bloody hell, Jack, he's been coming in for months. Older gentleman? Comes in at eight-twenty every morning, yes? Anyway, what's with all these flowers? It's like bloody Kew Gardens in here."

There were flowers on every table and more located on the shelves above the counter.

"Can I not spruce the place up a bit? It needs a bit of cheer and the customers like them."

"Oh, right. So an attractive florist moves in next door and all of a sudden you're Monty Don?"

"Yeah, it is a bit obvious. I'm running out of excuses to go next door, I've already brought her two coffees in."

"She'll be taking a restraining order out on you soon, saying that, if you keep buying her stock and giving her free coffee. You can take one of these brochures over for her — did she not say that her grandmother would like to go?"

Jack snatched the brochure, ruffled his hair and vanished, leaving Emma to contend with the morning rush, which currently consisted of two people.

Emma reflected on her morning as she cleared away the dishes. What if she hadn't called on Derek when she did? The thought filled her with a sense of dread, and she wondered how many other people were out there, just like him. She looked at the brochure for the social club and her visit with Derek affirmed her desire to help and that there were lonely people out there.

Postman Pete had obviously been, judging by the pile of post which sat, unloved, next to the till. One letter stood out from the rest as it had been opened. A bright red shone out as a contrast to the white paper, and on first glance it looked like a child's drawing. Among her numerous other roles, she had adopted the role of filing clerk so felt no guilt in prying open the letter and digesting the content. She was visibly shocked as Jack skipped back in.

"Her grandmother will be there Emma, and the good news is that Hayley wants to come as well. You're a genius!"

Emma held the letter above her head. "We might not have anywhere to host our new club, judging by the content of the letter. Jack, I think the landlady might be reaching the end of her tether with us?"

"Ah, Jasmine will be fine. As long as I throw a few crumbs her way each week, she'll be fine."

"Jack! Let me read this to you. *Jack, if you do not pay what you owe, I'll smash your face in and throw your stuff into the street.*"

"She'll be fine, she doesn't mean it!" said Jack, with an air of confidence.

"Jack, it's written in blood!"

"I know, it's quite impressive. I thought it was my lovely ex, Helen, at first. Anyway, it's lipstick, isn't it?"

"Whatever! She has still gone out of her way to make it look like blood. I think we've stretched her patience. How much rent do we owe at the moment?"

Jack shrugged his shoulders as he rolled his eyes skyward, his mouth moving as he worked the figures out in his head. "About four thousand. It's not the end of the world. Anyway, we owe the VAT man more than that and you don't see him sending me letters written in blood!"

Emma placed her head on the counter and feigned a sobbing sound. "Jack, we're screwed. Do you have any savings?"

"I did," he replied. "But the lovely Helen cleared me out of that as well."

"Look," said Emma. "I've got about eighteen hundred, maybe two thousand pounds saved. I was going to use it to go to Mexico, but we can give it to Jasmine to keep her off our backs for a bit."

"Okay," said Jack, without hesitation.

"Do you want to think about it first?" asked Emma sarcastically. "Bloody hell, you were nearly snatching the money out of my purse."

"There's no time for chivalry, Emma. Anyway, things will turn around. I'll get the front looking nice, we'll get the coffin-dodgers in, and the cash will be rolling in."

Emma did not look convinced as Jack waved goodbye to the two remaining customers. "Emma, I've been meaning to mention this for a while. You're more than just a friend or employee…"

"You can stop there, Jack," she interrupted. "If you're about to ask me out on a date, you can fuck right off."

"Firstly, Emma, I wasn't about to ask you out on a date, but it's good to know where I'd stand if I did. No, I was going to say that you're more than an employee, and I'd like to give you a share of the business. Ten percent!"

"Forty percent!" demanded Emma.

"Forty bloody percent? You're only putting two thousand pounds in! You've been watching too much of that *Dragons' Den* programme!" He paused for a few moments. "Oh, go on, then. It's forty percent of nothing at the end of the day anyway. But if you're a major shareholder, you can deal with that bloodsucker Jasmine!"

Emma scrunched the letter into a ball and threw it at Jack. "Sure thing, partner! This time next year, we'll be millionaires!"

Chapter Four

I'm Andy," said the slim but muscularly-built man with an air of confidence. His grey suit was immaculate, with just the slightest hint of a purple pinstripe that was easily overlooked. He ran his fingers through his styled brown hair and held a glass of red wine in his other hand. He was good-looking, and the approach would have raised a warmer reception had it not been nearly 9 p.m. As he smiled it was evident from the staining on his teeth that he'd been on the 'vino' since work. He casually leaned on the chest-height table like a horse peering out of a stable, and the odour of stale alcohol caused Emma to gag. "Can I buy you a drink?" he continued.

"Andy, it's nice to meet you, but I'm waiting for someone, so, you know…" she replied, politely, but with no doubt in her tone.

"Come on, let me buy you a drink. A good-looking girl like you shouldn't be sat on her own. I'm Andy."

"Yes… Andy, I got the name the first time. That's very kind, but really, I'm just waiting for someone."

"I sold three houses this week," he announced, in an irritating manner clearly meant to impress. "Over a million quid in sales, all… down… to… yours truly," he said, extending both thumbs and pointing towards himself.

"That's great, Andy. If I need to sell a house, I'll know exactly where to go," said Emma, with an increasing impatience that was lost on her inebriated suitor.

"You're selling your house?" asked Andy, as he moved his ear closer to Emma.

"No, I said…" she shook her head and pushed her chair further back. "Look, it doesn't matter, Andy. My friend will be here in a moment, so really, if you don't mind…"

Andy stood looking gormless and judging by the sound of heckling his progress was being scrutinised by three other 'half-cut' men stood by the bar. Undeterred, he extended his left arm so that the arm of his jacket moved to reveal a polished steel watch. "Rolex," he said, looking over the rim of his designer black glasses. He was met with a blank stare, and as he looked at his watch he raised his eyebrows quickly in succession.

"Listen, Andy, I think you're the third one of your 'gang' that's come over to me in the last ten minutes. I was polite and cordial to all of you and told you that I'm here to meet someone. I presume that bunch of imbeciles over there are your mates? Anyway, you've obviously spent a great deal of money on that gaudy-looking trinket on your wrist, so you'll know what time it is. Andy, it's time to fuck off."

He nodded as if the culmination of the conversation was his choice, and as he turned back towards his friends, he mouthed the word *lesbian*.

It was the first time she'd been into town on a Friday for months and the location was not of her choosing. The wine bar was right in the middle of the financial district and it always attracted the obnoxious office workers that were so polite in the coffee shop during the day, but rude and often aggressive when fuelled by expensive wine. She hadn't intended to stay out late which increased her frustration as she looked at her watch. She was underdressed in a white t-shirt tucked into black jeans, but her pretty face was captivating and male attention was not uncommon.

Jayne approached like a whirlwind, throwing her oversized handbag and black coat over the chair opposite Emma. "I know I'm useless, sorry Emma, I was late getting home, I couldn't get a taxi... anyway, how are you? God, you look beautiful, are you wearing makeup? You're not even wearing makeup, are you? It's not fair, I spend hours to look like this and you don't make an effort and you look like that," she said, at pace.

"Breathe," said Emma, slowly.

"I know, it's just been manic and I'm in dire need of a large gin. White wine?"

Jayne disappeared to the bar as quickly as she'd arrived. Emma smiled; her life always felt a little more in control in the company of Jayne, who was always wired. She worked in sales for a large manufacturer and her temperament was perfect for that environment.

"One large glass of wine for you, cheers!"

Emma raised an eyebrow of disapproval as the contents of the wine glass were almost spilling over the rim. "This doesn't look like a small glass! I've got work tomorrow."

"It's Saturday tomorrow!"

"People still drink coffee on a Saturday."

"Eyes right," said Jayne, flicking her hair seductively. "Three suits looking directly over at us."

Emma shook her head. "Trust me on this, Jayne. A bunch of drunken arseholes. I've already had the pleasure of their finest banter."

"Oh, well. It's a bit busy in here, Emma. Why did you choose here?"

"Me?" laughed Emma. "This was all your idea."

The contents of the gin were soon drained and quickly replaced, as Emma nursed her goblet of wine. The remnants of the office crowd had moved on, replaced by the evening crowd.

"So?" asked Emma.

Jayne looked deliberately vague. "What?"

"You bloody well know what, Jayne. I don't come out into town if I can help it. Even my oldest friend telling me she had life-changing news still made me think twice. Are you pregnant?"

"Predictable, Emma, too predictable. Just because a woman has exciting news doesn't mean they're pregnant. Anyway, if I was pregnant, I'd be suing Ann Summers for paternity."

"Okay, so not pregnant. Moving house?"

"Ooh, warm, of sorts," said Jayne, as she took a drink. She placed the glass carefully on the table and theatrically extended her arms. "I am leaving this fair Island and moving to Singapore."

Emma frowned as she processed the information. "You're not… you can't. When?"

"Six weeks. Work has asked me to go out there for two years to head up their regional sales office. But that's not the good bit."

"I didn't think that was good," said Emma.

Jayne ignored her and returned her hands to the table. She moved her head closer to Emma. "You're coming with me," she said, as she rapidly clapped the tips of her fingers together.

"How much gin have you drank?" asked Emma.

"I'm serious. Work assumes that most people who relocate are married or have a significant other so factor in flights and accommodation for two. I'm not married so I asked if you could be my significant other. They said yes!"

"I can't go. What about work?"

"You're working in a coffee shop? Emma, you've got a degree in economics!"

Emma nodded. "All that degree did was give me four years to realise how much I hated economics!"

Jayne tilted her head in a slightly condescending manner. "But you're thirty-five."

"Thirty-four!" said Emma. "Besides, I don't just work there, I'm now a shareholder and I'm doing something I like!"

"Emma, I love you like a sister, but you're working in a crappy little shop. You're single with no kids. You can move to Singapore and use that degree to earn some serious money. We'll have a ball."

"I know, but it's not that simple. There is someone."

Jayne looked troubled. "Who, and why have you never mentioned him?"

Emma was reluctant. "It's complicated and I knew what you'd say," she said, lowering her head like a guilty dog.

"You're going to have to tell me now," said Jayne.

Emma rested her head in her hands. "It's Jack."

"Who's Jack?" asked Jayne. "Wait, not Jack... *Jack*? Please, Emma. Please tell me it's not Jack from work."

Emma looked forlorn, like she was confessing to a schoolyard crush. "Yes, it's Jack from work."

Jayne arched her back. "I think I need another gin. How long has this been going on? I thought he had a girlfriend?"

"He did, but they broke up. There is nothing going on, but he thinks we're just friends. There is this other girl he likes now, as well," she said, dropping her shoulders.

"Emma, don't get me wrong. Jack is a nice guy and all that, but you're, well, stunning. You could have your pick of any man in here. He's just, well... Jack. A bit of a buffoon. I don't mean to be harsh, Emma. But this is a staggering opportunity, don't waste it."

Emma knew she was right. Where was her life going? It was something she'd often pondered but she'd become complacent. The Jack issue was as bewildering to her as it was to Jayne. When he was with Helen, it'd never entered her head. It was only when they were breaking up that she noticed another side of him. She convinced herself it was a phase, that it'd pass. But it hadn't.

"Jayne, it sounds amazing. Let me think about it?"

"Of course you can. Don't let Jack get in the way of this chance, Emma, and remember, it's only for two years."

Emma stared at her drink and pushed her finger around the lipstick covered rim. She looked at Jayne and shook her head. "I don't know what's going on. How have I fallen in love with an oaf like Jack?"

Chapter Five

The ageing Vespa was struggling; something didn't feel as it should. Aesthetically she'd seen better days, but the engine had never missed a beat. Home was along a promenade two miles long which ran parallel to the charming Douglas coastline. Toward the end of the sandy expanse was the formidable Summer Hill, a long and arduous climb towards home in Onchan. As a child, Jack would cycle along the promenade at pace, to carry sufficient momentum for the climb ahead. All but a few would succumb by the first corner, where a convenient and welcome bench lay; the single-geared BMX would be dismounted, and the remainder of the journey would be completed on foot. Jack always smiled as he passed the bench, but now, twenty or so horsepower provided the thrust, rather than tired legs. His confidence that his ageing steed would continue to make it further than the bench was starting to wane. He willed the bike up the remainder of the hill and took a mental note to take a slightly less abrupt route home. On a warm evening in June, the Isle of Man was one of the finest places you could hope to live. The pleasant breeze and an open-faced helmet brought a contented smile to Jack's face, with the wind up the leg of his shorts an added bonus.

The left rear indicator was currently out of order, so he raised his left hand to take him onto his grandad's road, which, was another sharp climb. Jack would be the first to acknowledge his deficiencies when it came to sporting fashion, but the sight that greeted him at the foot of the hill caused even him to stare in bewilderment. He was drawn to the 1970's style tennis shorts which would be considered tight, bordering on obscene. The back of his knees were barely visible, all but covered by stretched white socks — a contrast to the black formal shoes. The ensemble was completed with a less-than-fetching off-white vest. Jack was about to scoff when he recalled his initial efforts at exercise, and his sneer turned quickly to admiration.

"What... the... fuck," he said, slowly. He pulled the bike to the side of the road and jumped off, removing his helmet. He walked up the road and soon caught the man jogging a smidgen quicker than walking pace. "Oi, what the hell are you doing! Grandad! Hey, you crazy bugger, it's me, Jack!"

Geoffrey didn't break his stride, continuing his journey up the hill towards his bungalow. "I'm not stopping, Jack, I've been trying to make it up this bloody hill all week."

Jack walked behind, but with enough distance to avoid a direct association to the man in front. The only saving grace for Geoffrey was that he was jogging; if he were dressed like that and walking, he would surely have been arrested by now. Two schoolchildren on the opposite side of the road looked over in astonishment as he ever so slowly moved up the hill. "Go on, Rocky!" shouted one of the boys, causing Geoffrey to punch the air in acknowledgement. His pace slowed further as the incline increased, but to Jack's surprise he continued to push on. It'd been years since Jack walked up the hill and he'd forgotten how challenging it was. "C'mon, Grandad!" he shouted, as he approached the crest of the hill.

Geoffrey stood by his front path and placed his hands on his hips, looking proudly back to where he'd just climbed. "What are you doing, Grandad?" asked Jack.

Geoffrey puffed out his cheeks as he caught his breath. "I'm on my way to Wimbledon, what's it bloody look like I'm doing? I'm getting fit."

"You're a bit…"

"What? Old?" barked Geoffrey.

"No. Well, yes, of course you are. No, I was going to say a little… revealing. You've already been nicked once this week, you don't want to add a charge of indecent exposure to your expanding 'rap sheet' do you?"

"Your mum told me about this dating club for pensioners you've set up. I'm trying to get a bit more buff before I go."

"Well, it's more of a social club, Grandad."

"So it's not a dating club?"

"Well, not specifically. I don't want to end up as Cilla Black for the infirm."

"I've told them all down at the legion that it's a dating club. I've got about fifteen people wanting to come."

Jack's eyes widened. "Fifteen, that's good. What are they expecting, though? They don't think I've set up some knocking shop, do they?"

"Don't be bloody stupid. Well, Dirty Eric did ask, but he didn't get his nickname for nothing. They just want to meet other people, and if there were a few attractive ladies who wanted their dance card stamped, well, even better. That's why I want to be in peak condition. I feel fit — the doctor gave my blood pressure the clean bill of health as well."

"Good! That's what I was coming to check on, make sure you actually went. Does the doctor know you've taken up running?"

"No, but he did say gentle exercise was good."

"I'm not sure this is what he had in mind. If you're serious about getting fit, we need to get you something to wear. Seriously, Grandad, you can't go out looking like that. I'll take you shopping for something more appropriate."

❧

"This is it, Horace. Time to see if all the hard work is paying off."

Jack had been to the gym every morning; it was something he now looked forward to. The muscle pain had dulled, and he was now on a first-name basis with the staff. He stood in the exact spot where he first discovered his breasts and removed his t-shirt. He cupped them and sure enough, they'd reduced. He pulled his mobile phone from his pocket and examined a picture he'd taken a week ago. His chest had reduced and the 'muffin tops' at the side of his waist had shrank.

"How can Hayley resist that, Horace?" said Jack, flexing his biceps. He was eating healthier and sleeping better as he wasn't drinking. He felt good and his efforts in the gym were starting to pay dividends.

"We'll be out of this shithole soon, Horace," said Jack, collapsing onto his sofa. He chuckled to himself as he thought about his grandad. He'd taken a sneaky picture as he ran up the hill and texted it through to Emma, with the caption:

> Me in 20 years? Grandad's taken up running! X
> ps, how's the hangover?

He re-read the letter from the estate agents and looked around the flat. He strained his face as he realised it wasn't that bad. The main issue was the memories of Helen. This was their flat and this was their dream, one that was quickly shattered when she met Jerry from work. He was completely over Helen, but the flat was a constant reminder. He'd never made the connection about his weight gain and the sudden interest in Jerry. Was she really that shallow?

The phone vibrated on his lap:

> Well done, Grandad! He still looks better than your first attempt. Hangover awful. Going to bed, see you Monday X

The letter from the estate agent served as one month's notice on the flat. He'd been willing this day for months, but a wave of panic hit him; he would soon be homeless. He didn't have any money other than his deposit on the flat and the Vespa was about to pack in. The shop was on the bones of its arse and needed new customers or, in reality, he doubted they'd see the end of the summer out. He texted Emma to tell her about the fifteen punters Grandad had rounded up. He knew he needed to get on board with this initiative otherwise he'd be going to the jobcentre, and he knew he was far from a desired candidate.

He'd always seen the shop as Helen's dream and a small part of him harboured a desire to see it fail. It was irrational; Helen had long since moved on and the only person that failure would hurt was him and Emma. The shop was more than work; it was like a micro-community. People genuinely cared about it — the majority, a lot more than Jack. He'd taken Emma for granted for too long. She was forever coming up with wacky ideas to drum up business, which he'd often dismiss without consideration. She was on minimum wage which she didn't always take if the shop was short; she put her heart into making it a success and she'd be devastated if it failed. He didn't know if it related to feeling fitter, but he was motivated like no other time in his life. He was part of something that he'd miss if it were taken away. His approach to the shop had been the same as the approach to his waistline — one of blissful ignorance that bordered on neglect.

Being outside early on a Sunday morning was a novelty. Normally, Jack would be sleeping off the previous night's excess and watching repeats of *Columbo* all afternoon. He awoke with a sense of purpose and motivation that took him outside on his day off. Things that would usually irritate — such as the flat — somehow seemed a little more bearable. Even the terminally ill Vespa burst into life at the first time of asking. The sun glistened off the tranquil sea and the promenade was packed with people taking advantage of the glorious weather. It was a child's paradise, with two miles of uninterrupted walkway which provided the ultimate test for a young cyclist. There was a unique smell that carried in the wind on a day like this — sea salt mixed with fresh seaweed — and it conjured fond memories of sandcastles and ice cream. Growing up in a seaside resort was a privilege, and through a child's eyes, it never rained and the beaches were always full to capacity. The Isle of Man was not immune to the effects of mass tourism and had seen a steady decline in visitor numbers over the years. Guesthouses had given way to executive flats, and the sound of funfairs and bingo callers had long since vanished. There was always a sense of melancholy when he rode along the promenade — thinking of how it once was — but this was eased as he looked at the happy families enjoying their day.

There were people milling about as he pulled up outside the shop. Emma had suggested opening on Sundays, but he'd given the idea short shrift; he was starting to reconsider. He stood in front of the expanse of glass and took a few steps backward. There was no sugar-coating it — the shop, as it was, was an eyesore. It was by far the worst in the street, and the flaking black paint now had a dull grey look to it. He took the pile of sandpaper and the scraper, paint, and brushes from his backpack, and moved forward with purpose. He wasn't proficient at DIY, as the angled curtain pole in his flat would attest, but he was determined to give the shop every fighting chance of survival. He only hoped his efforts were not too late.

The morning soon disappeared, and he was only disturbed by the occasional comment of, "missed a bit," by a passing joker — funny the first time, but quickly worn out. The classic anthems on his phone kept the spring in his step and as he stood back to admire his handiwork, he was frustrated with himself for leaving it so long. Not only was it an easy job, it was enjoyable, and the difference in a lick of paint was staggering. All he needed now was a 'J' for the sign.

He was proud of his efforts, and the first person he wanted to tell was Emma. He sent her a picture with the message:

> Only took me 4 years! I'm one lazy bastard. It's the start of a new me X This time next year we'll be millionaires, partner! X

None of the shops in the street were open, so Jack was surprised to see lights in the locksmiths. They hadn't seen Ray since he'd been taken away in the ambulance and even Postman Pete hadn't heard anything. He was an unhealthy specimen and they speculated that they wouldn't see him again. Jack moved closer and the door was slightly ajar. He looked around but the street was desolate. He rushed to put his helmet on for protection, and he held his scraper in an offensive manner.

"Hello, Ray. It's Jack. Are you there?"

There was no response, so he called out again, moving forward cautiously. "Ray, it's Jack from across the road."

He gagged as the scent of stale alcohol hit him; it was an obstacle course of discarded bottles. He used the scraper to push food wrappers from the counter next to the till, causing a rancid sandwich to fall to the floor. He jumped back as a muffled groan came from behind the door at the rear of the shop. He raised the scraper and tightened the straps on his helmet. "I'm armed!" he shouted, with a shaking voice. "Come out!"

He gingerly opened the door and peered into the room; the small frosted glass window provided a nominal amount of light. It took a moment for his eyes to adjust, but through the darkness a silhouette could be seen stooped over the worktop, right hand shaking vigorously. Jack retreated in disgust. "Ray, It's Jack. I did knock, several times!"

Ray spun 'round. "Bloody hell, Jack! You could have given me another heart attack, you stupid bugger!"

"Did I catch you at an awkward time?" said Jack, with a childish smirk.

Ray paused for a moment before it dawned on him what Jack was on about. "I'm shaking my tin of soup, you mucky bugger! The chance for the other would be a fine thing. At my age, I'd need a stiff north-easterly breeze and a bicycle pump. I'm softer than a wet biscuit these days."

"Thanks for that, Ray. Your door is wide open, I thought you were a burglar."

"It's a shop, lad. The door is supposed to be open."

"But it's Sunday, Ray. And, to be fair, we thought you might be..."

"Dead?"

"No. Well, yes, a little bit. How are you, anyway?"

"Never better. Until you scared the hell out of me. Touch of high blood pressure caused a funny turn. Doctor's said to lay off the booze and get some exercise."

Jack picked up two empty bottles. "Ah, the sobriety going well, then?"

"Have to start somewhere, Jack."

The room was full of rubbish and empty bottles. Ray looked sheepish, as he struggled to pick up a discarded bottle. "Let me," said Jack. "You make your soup and I'll sort this lot out."

Jack was sorry to see him in this state. They weren't close, but he liked him; he was a similar generation to his grandad, and very funny. Not funny that your mum would approve of, mind, but bawdy, like a 1970's workingman's club comedian. He was well-built for his age, with broad shoulders and a well-worn face — clearly an ox of a man in his youth, but there were signs of frailty. His bulbous nose was pockmarked and reddened, his eyes were sunken and tinged with yellow.

The smell of stale red wine was making Jack ill. "We'd make a fortune if we could return these bottles, Ray. Fair play to you, that's an impressive collection."

Ray was taken aback at the number of bottles, now neatly placed into several shopping bags. "I wasn't always like this, Jack. I didn't touch a drop for twenty years."

"You're certainly making up for it now?"

"Aye, son," said Ray, sitting on a delicate wooden stool. "Every time I've turned to the drink there's a woman involved. Stay away from them, Jack. Nothing but bloody trouble. My first wife left me, I hit the drink hard. Same with my second and third."

"Why did they leave you?" asked Jack.

Ray was pensive. "Probably because of the drink, son."

"How was there a woman involved in the latest sobriety relapse?" asked Jack. "I thought you were single?"

Ray chuckled at the thought of a woman in his life. "I'm single, son, but I can see how you wouldn't be certain. I'm a prize catch, after all. No, this is what you could call a long-distance relationship with two American sisters, Candy and Charity."

Jack's interest was piqued, and he placed the final empty bottle on the worktop. "Now that is the perfect start to an anecdote, Ray. Please… do continue!"

"It was about six months ago, just a few days before Christmas, and the phone rang. That was strange enough because I'd forgotten I owned a phone. This bubbly voice on the phone introduced herself as Candy, or Charity — one or the other. She said she'd phoned me by accident and chatted for a few moments. She told me where she lived and how she worked for one of the big, fancy, finance companies. She said goodbye and I didn't think any more about it. A couple of days later the phone rang and it was her, again. She told me how nice it'd been talking, and she told me a bit more about herself, how she and her sister worked together as investment advisors. She made out that it was fate that she'd called me by accident. Anyway, she started talking to me about stocks and shares and how her clients were making a fortune."

Jack frowned, placing his elbows on the countertop. "I'm guessing this story didn't finish with the happy ending I first thought it was going to?"

"What she said seemed to make sense. Well, no, in fact it didn't. I hadn't a bloody clue what she was talking about, other than a lot of people were making a load of money out of their advice. It started quite small as she said she wanted to prove how good she was before I committed too much. I bought a couple of hundred shares in a new company — something to do with the internet — and in a couple of days I'd made two hundred pounds profit. Then her sister phones me and repeats the same charm offensive. I was blinded by the flattery. They made me feel like I was some sort of intelligent, shrewd investor, where in fact I didn't have a bloody clue what they were on about. I was blinded by two attractive-sounding women."

Ray pushed himself to his feet and reached for a tatty-looking blue-ring binder on top of a small wooden desk. "Take a look."

Jack thumbed through a pile of paper more than two inches thick. There were a multitude of share certificates, each with the name of a different company. "I've never heard of any of these companies?" said Jack.

"You won't have, son. That's because they don't exist. The bank phoned me in the end due to all of these transactions that were going through. The sisters told me they'd do this and to tell them it was none of their business. Which I did. The bank eventually phoned the police who explained how it was all a big scam — I think they call it a boiler room."

Jack shook his head and thought of what had happened to Derek. "Are all old people a bit gullible?"

"No, son. We're just from a generation where we look for the best in people."

"How much did you lose?" asked Jack.

"Just over thirty thousand," he replied.

Jack slowly mouthed the words *FUCK'N HELL*.

"That's not the best of it, son. A few days after the bank and police told me there was nothing they could do, the phone rang again. This time it was a man with a very formal English accent. He told me how he worked for a firm of solicitors who were recovering money from the company who'd ripped me off. He said the FBI had seized all of their records which is how they'd got my details. He said my money was safe and it was in a frozen bank account. All I needed to do was employ the law firm and they'd get my money back plus they'd recover any legal fees I'd paid out."

"Please tell me you didn't," pleaded Jack.

"I was desperate, and this seemed the only way to get my money back."

"How much did you give them?"

Ray rubbed his weather forehead in frustration. "Eleven thousand pounds."

"No!" said Jack. "I'm guessing you didn't get your money back?"

"Did I, bollocks. It was only when they kept phoning me back for more money that I twigged on. I have to admit, they are clever bastards, though. Talk about taking advantage.

The police said they'd look into it, but pretty much told me my money was gone. So, thanks to Candy and Charity I started drinking again and ended up in hospital."

Jack placed the folder back onto the desk. "That's an expensive folder you've got there. I have to say, they are pretty ingenious, especially the follow-up scam. I bet loads of people fall for that, though."

"That's what the police said. There are hundreds across the UK and at least eight in the Isle of Man. Sadly, most of them are older people who aren't getting interest on their savings, so are easily persuaded to move their cash into seemingly, safe investments. The police have put notices in the paper but there is only so much they can do."

"You won't lose your house?" asked Jack.

"No, son. It just means that I'll be working in here till they carry me out in a box."

"Come on, you stupid old bugger," said Jack. "I'll help you get this place cleaned up. Nobody is going to come in here with it looking like this."

Ray was grateful, not only for the help but also the company. He lived alone so being in the shop was the only time he saw other people. It'd been a difficult few months and losing the money was horrible, but even worse and the thing he couldn't get over was how he had been so easily taken in. He felt humiliated and despite the reassurances of the police, he felt vulnerable.

Jack closed his fingers and held his hand outstretched. "Ray, see this?"

Ray looked confused. "What?"

Jack shook his fist. "Magic beans, Ray. You can have them for only a tenner!"

Ray laughed for the first time in an age. "Cheeky sod. You should have gone higher, I'd have given you twenty!"

Chapter Six

Postman Pete flew into the shop with his usual gusto. "Happy Monday, you beautiful specimens! The sun is shining and it's a wonderful day!"

"Someone's happy, Pete. Your blind date didn't disappoint, then?" asked Emma.

"It did not!" exclaimed Pete, as he twirled Emma's black hair which, for once, wasn't tied back. "In fact, he exceeded expectations — in every department! You're looking rather glam, for a Monday morning, are you not, Emma?"

"Enough information, and you know a girl likes to make an effort from time to time."

"Look at him," said Emma. "God, he's such a loser!"

Jack was at the front of the shop clearing tables and caught his reflection in the shop window. He was wearing a close-fitting polo shirt, and rather than wincing, he was turning like a rotisserie chicken, admiring himself from every angle.

"Here, Pete, you'd definitely have a go of this, now wouldn't you?" asked Jack. "It's not perfect, but it's getting there."

"Jack, darling, I'd ride you like a rodeo bull."

"Aww, thanks, Pete, that means a lot," said Jack, with a proud expression. "I hope Hayley shares your enthusiasm."

"Well, she is in here every five minutes," said Emma. "She must drink ten coffees a day, and you don't even charge her!"

"She gave us these flowers," replied Jack. "And I noticed the ones she'd left on the counter seem to have mysteriously vanished and I'm guessing are now sat in your flat?"

"Oh, speak of the devil and who should appear," said Emma, as Hayley waved enthusiastically through the large windows.

"Morning all," she said. "And what a beautiful one it is. Pete, have you hurt your leg? I noticed you were walking a bit awkwardly."

Pete's cheeks flushed as he diverted the question. "What a wonderful bouquet, are they for me?"

"Sadly not, Pete," replied Hayley. "These are the finest yellow roses, and if my memory serves me correct, Emma, also your favourite flower?"

"Oh, they're stunning, Hayley, thank you!" said Emma, who now felt a tinge of guilt for being a little malevolent earlier. "Can I get you your usual?"

"Oh, that would be wonderful, thank you. Good morning, Jack!"

Jack grinned like a docile teenager. "Morning, Hayley, you look...." He was captivated by her glistening blue eyes. Her hair was a golden blonde bob that bounced off her shoulders. She even smelt lovely. It was a scent he'd never come across before; it reminded him of the candy floss machine at the fair. She was elegant, the type of woman who wouldn't look out of place in a Cary Grant film. She was the sort of lady that would ride an attractive bicycle with a large basket on the front which contained a fresh picnic, ready to be unravelled at a moment's notice. She'd stop periodically to pick up a wildflower and cute animals would congregate for an audience with her.

"Jack, back in the room!" shouted Emma.

He jolted back to reality. "Pretty. I was going to say you look pretty."

Hayley looked a little uneasy as she took her coffee. "Thanks… Jack. Before I go, can I have a really quick word?"

She took him to the front of the shop, and as much as Emma arched her neck, she wasn't able to eavesdrop. In desperation, she looked to Pete — who, unfortunately, was equally uninformed.

"Thank you for the roses, Hayley, they're beautiful!" shouted Emma, as the door closed.

Pete slow-clapped Jack. "Smooth, my friend, very smooth. I'm not sure that could have been any more cringe-worthy."

Jack was fit to burst. "Well, I must have done something right."

Emma lurched forward. "What? Why? What do you mean?"

Jack held out as long as he could. "She wants to see me. She wants to meet me for a drink after work!"

"No way!" said Emma. "Go you!" Her voice was wavering slightly, and she immediately excused herself.

"Check me out," said Jack, flexing his arms. "It must be the new and improved guns."

Emma was deflated; several of her regular customers commented on it, but she brushed it off as 'feeling under the weather.' She was pleased to see Jack happy; he was due some good fortune. As soon as the shop emptied from the lunchtime flurry, Jack grabbed his keys and took Emma by the hand. "I need a favour," he said, ushering her through the front door.

"Where are we going?" she protested.

"I need a new shirt, and let's face it, my fashion sense is—"

"Shit," said Emma.

"I was going for eclectic, but *shit* works."

Jack marched her with verve towards Marks & Spencer. "Seriously, no," said Emma. "If you're after a nice shirt we need to go somewhere else." The wicked side of her wanted him to buy something a bit naff, but she also wanted him to look his best; she knew he really liked Hayley.

She took the lead and brought him into a large shop that was littered with designer brands. Jack was impressed but aghast, as he looked at the price tag on the first shirt she picked out, A hundred and ten pounds, holy shit, Emma."

"Do you want to look nice or look like a vagrant?"

"Here, you go into that changing room and I'll bring you a few over to try on. What size? Medium?"

"A generous medium. Call it a large to be on the safe side," said Jack.

Jack sat in the small changing room and pulled over the wafer-thin green curtain. He didn't like shopping for clothes; it made him anxious. He undressed and shuffled uncomfortably on the white bench seat as he looked at his watch; there was something about dressing rooms he didn't trust. His eyes scoured the room, looking for a hidden camera or any other form of covert voyeurism — he wondered if this mistrust was as a result of his own perverted mind. He strained his eyes towards a black hole in the bottom left corner. *Dirty bastards,* he thought, moving closer. There was a narrow hole — small, but big enough to accommodate a tiny camera. He couldn't get a clear view from his seated position, so he crouched down, first on one leg, and then he fell onto his knees. He moved his head into the gap between the end of the seat and the exterior wall, but it was still difficult to get a clear view. He stretched his hand and extended his middle finger, but it was too thick. He prodded with his little finger, which fit snuggly into the tight hole. The wall was a thin layer of plywood and it became quickly obvious that the hole was redundant, perhaps from a previous shop fitting. As he tried to retract his finger he realised — to his complete horror — that it was stuck. He composed himself and tried again, but it was useless. The more he pulled his finger, the rolls of skin would form and prevent exit. *Shit,* he thought, trying to manoeuvre his other hand to assist, but the lack of space and angle he was knelt meant assistance was impossible. He pushed and pulled his hand, but the scruffy edges of the drill hole were ripping into his skin. His shopping anxiety was amplified, and he could feel the sweat dripping down his face.

"Jack, I've got four shirts to try, three I like but the other I'm not too sure about, but see what you think," said Emma, through the curtain.

"Jack?"

"Eh, just a minute, Emma, I'm just getting undressed," replied Jack, who was now very uncomfortable.

Emma paced outside for a few moments. "What you are doing in there?"

"Nothing," responded Jack, through gritted teeth. "Emma," he said finally, in desperation. "I think I'm stuck."

"What do you mean, *stuck?* Okay, I'm coming in, make sure you're decent."

She slowly pulled open the curtain and as she peered around, she was greeted by the vision of Jack kneeling in front of her with his rear end directly in her eye line. "Holy fuck, Jack. What the hell are you doing down there?"

"I got my finger stuck in a hole."

"But… you're fucking naked," she said, in a state of bewilderment. "Why are you naked and why have you got your finger in a hole?"

"I thought it was a camera. And I told you, *I don't do underpants.*"

"Good god, Jack, can you not do anything that doesn't end up with you potentially being arrested or barred?"

She took his t-shirt and placed it over his bum which was now open and presented to her like a bloom on a summer's day. "I need to cover that before I come down there!" she said.

Emma struggled to get a view as the light was blocked by Jack. "Get your phone," said Jack. "And use the camera light."

"Okay," she said. "But this is a loan phone as my other one broke when I was out the other…"

"I'm sure the story of why you have a loan phone is enchanting, but right now, please help me get out of this hole. I was buying a shirt to get into a hole, *and it wasn't this fucking one!*"

"Okay, I'm trying!" She fumbled with the phone and frantically pressed buttons until a beam of light erupted from the rear. She cast the light towards Jack, but it was useless — there was nothing she could see. She manoeuvred the phone further and caught a glimpse of his hand which had now gone a painful shade of white as a solitary bead of blood ran down his wrist. As he pulled again, the shirt covering his bum fell to the floor, revealing his bare cheeks.

"I can't believe you've not got trousers on," whispered Emma.

"I was going to try new jeans on. I asked you to get jeans," said Jack.

"You didn't, you only asked for shirts," said Emma, who was now slightly offended.

"Do you think I would sit naked if I didn't ask you for jeans?" said Jack, getting more agitated. "What's that noise? Are you taking pictures of me?"

"What? No! If you could see what I can see, you'd understand why I'm not taking a picture of you."

The pinging sound continued, so she moved the screen to her face, which was filled with Jack's naked torso. She was confused, as the screen was covered with miniature 'thumbs-up' symbols. She panicked as the realisation set in. "Jack," she whispered. "Jack, please don't get mad."

"About what?" asked Jack. "I don't think things can get much worse."

"You know this phone is a loan phone?" said Emma.

"Yes, I remember you saying. It was an interesting conversation. Please, tell me about it again."

Emma twitched her nose like Samantha from *Bewitched*. "Well, the thing is, Jack, in my rush to turn the light on, I think I may have also turned Facebook Live on."

"What's Facebook Live?" said Jack, with a tinge of panic in his voice.

"Well," said Emma, "Imagine I had the ability to live-stream what I'm looking at to all of my friends, instantly."

"Please tell me you're joking?" pleaded Jack.

"No. But the good news is you've had forty-six likes."

"That's pretty good," said Jack. "You'll need to show me the video when they release me from jail."

"Wait there," said Emma.

"Well, I'm not bloody going anywhere, am I!" snapped Jack.

Emma opened the curtain and moved around the corner to see a changing room on the other side of the wall. Fortunately, the room was empty, and Emma moved to open a small cupboard in the bottom corner; she could see his finger, which had visibly swelled. "I'm going to try and push it. Stand by."

She gently pushed the reddened digit and as soon as she did, she could hear a groan of pain through the wall.

"I've got an idea!" said Emma, darting to retrieve her handbag. She returned to the other dressing room. "I've got a lip balm," she said, loud enough so Jack could hear.

The pain in Jack's knees was becoming uncomfortable so he shuffled as best as he could to distribute the pressure. His bum moved in unison with his knees and as he gyrated the curtain opened. An elegant older woman with styled silver hair stood, perplexed by the vision before her.

Jack was in too much pain to appreciate that he now had company. "Make sure I'm properly lubed up before you start pushing it in," he demanded.

Emma pushed and Jack pulled; in a wonderful instant, his finger was removed from its incarceration. As the finger released, he fell sideways and landed on his back in a crumpled, sweating heap. His relief was short-lived when he looked up and saw the horrified lady looking down on him. "Morning. I'm not even going to try and explain this one," he said.

"Bloody deviant!" she said, in disgust.

"We need to get out of here," said Emma, helping him to his seat. "And put your bloody jeans back on."

"I can't go, I need a new shirt for tonight!" he said, in desperation.

Emma had forgotten why they were there, and the recollection saddened her. "Okay, try them on and I'll come back in a few minutes."

She looked at dresses she couldn't possibly afford and the thought of Jack going on a date filled her with dismay. She was irritated that she'd not done anything about her feelings, but in reality the attraction was as much as a surprise to her. Her phone continued to beep and the video was now up to 108 likes. *He is such a loser,* she said to herself, with a smile. Jack was a klutz; he couldn't do anything without it ending up in a drama of sort, but she liked that. She could see it would get embarrassing, but Jack didn't care, so why should she? Hayley was lovely but she knew she had to tell Jack how she felt, at least then he would have all of the facts.

She stomped back to the dressing room and took a deep breath. "Look, I need to tell you something," she said, with an uneasy voice. "You might find this a bit weird, so, my apologies in advance. I don't think you should go out with

Hayley. I know you like her, but… the thing is, I like you. I didn't always, in fact. I used to think you were a bit of a dick. Still do, sometimes. I don't know how, why, or when, but I do. Like you, that is. I like being with you, I like working with you. We can turn the shop around and we'll have fun doing it. You're an embarrassment, but I like that — you make me laugh even when you don't mean to. How many people do you know that shit themselves at the gym, or lie naked in a changing room demanding that I lube him up with lip balm? There, I said it!"

Jack placed a pair of blue jeans on her shoulder at the same time as the curtain opened. The disgruntled, elegant, grey-haired lady appeared from behind the curtain in her new blouse, and said in her poshest voice, "You fucking perverts deserve each other!"

"Making friends, Emma?" asked Jack.

"I thought you were in there, you dick!" whispered Emma.

Jack pointed to his bag. "I bought this, and I'm returning these jeans."

"Let's go!" said Emma, as she grabbed his wrist. "Before we get thrown out."

Jack arrived early and took a seat by the window. The bar was empty apart from a group of women who looked like they'd been drinking for most of the afternoon. He was apprehensive but felt confident in his new white Hilfiger shirt. Hayley had chosen the most expensive wine bar in town and his wallet had still not recovered from earlier. He looked at the wine list and really hoped that she wasn't the wine drinking sort. He'd not been on a date of merit for a long time and he had a nervous feeling in his stomach that would soon be eased by the first pint of bitter. He took a large mouthful before he paced himself, the words of wisdom from Emma ringing through his mind: *Don't make a dick out of yourself, and don't get drunk.* She was right; Jack didn't need liquid help to make a fool of himself — that came all by itself. He played with his phone and tapped his feet as the minutes ticked by. The meeting time soon came and went and Jack was beginning to think he'd gone to the wrong place. His phone beeped, and he jumped on it like a fat kid on a cupcake. It was a text from Emma:

> Phone dying and no charge for the loan phone.
> Enjoy your night and remember, don't be a tool.
> Let me know how you get on 2moz. I'll open up,
> so you can have a drink. X

He smiled and took another mouthful of his beer knowing he could have a lie-in. *Perhaps I won't be alone,* he thought.

"I'm so sorry I'm late, Jack. I had to go around to check in on my grandmother. I hope I haven't kept you too long?"

She leaned over and gave him a kiss on the cheek. "Can I get you a drink?" asked Jack.

"Ohh, yes please," she said, picking up the wine list that Jack had placed deliberately out of sight. His fear was allayed when she asked for a mineral water.

Jack gave himself a pep talk as he stood at the bar. He ordered another pint and felt assured that two would be fine, *just take it easy*.

"You look lovely, Hayley," he said, handing her a drink. She was only wearing jeans and a stripy white top, but she looked classy. The top she wore for work was loose-fitting, and he hadn't noticed before now how fantastic her boobs were. She talked to him about her day, but as Jack looked intently into those lovely blue eyes he could feel his eyeballs being dragged down like a sinking ship. It was a physical battle to maintain eye contact and soon he was having an argument with himself in his head. He rubbed his eyes, but it was useless; it was like an incessant itch that was starting to burn the back of his eye socket. *Look down, you fool, she won't notice.*

Now he couldn't even hear her speak and the only way to ease the burning was to quickly look down. There, he thought, as his eyes darted up and down. She paused for a moment and looked at him with a strange expression. *Shit,* he thought. *She's seen me. Now she thinks I'm a pervert.* His fear was confirmed when she placed her elbows on the table and joined her hands, all but covering her chest.

Jack was tuned back in.

"So, Emma tells me you've been doing some great work with the elderly. You have your first event, next week?"

"Yes!" said Jack, enthusiastically. "Next Saturday night, we're having a tea dance. Emma's idea, in truth, but, should be good. I'll need to make sure I buy a new mop!" he said, but instantly regretted it.

"A mop?" asked Hayley, slightly confused.

He thought of saying nothing, but following the breast incident he had to follow through. "Yes…" he mumbled. "For all the, you know, piss. Erm… old people… mop…"

Hayley sat with her mouth agape as her eyebrows rose slightly. "Okay, so, I'm sure it'll be a huge success. I was telling my grandmother, but I think she's house-trained so you shouldn't need the mop for her."

"Great," said Jack. "It'll be in the cupboard, on standby."

For the love of God, stop talking, you huge, giant turd, he thought.

He moved on quickly. "So, the shop. How's it going? Busy, I hope? What got you into gardening?"

"It's going great, thank you. Still plenty of work to do but I'm getting a lot of regular customers, which is good. I have a distant cousin who got me into gardening at a young age. You may know him if you're into gardening programmes, he's often on the television."

"It's not that Alan Titwank, is it?" said Jack, laughing. *Jack, stop it, for the love of God, have a night off.* He could visualise Emma sat in the corner of the room shaking her head in despair.

Hayley was starting to look uncomfortable, and Jack's 'humour' was clearly lost on her. "No, it's Kelvin Reed."

"Shit, no way, he's your cousin?"

"Distant," said Hayley, unsure if Jack was being sarcastic.

"My mum loves him," continued Jack. "I bought her his calendar for Christmas and she has every book he's ever written!"

"Great," said Hayley. "That's my little claim to fame and the reason I got into gardening."

The conversation dried up and Jack nervously drained the contents of his glass. "Another drink? Something stronger?"

"No, but thanks," said Hayley, placing her hand over the top of her drink. "Thanks for coming tonight. You must be wondering why I asked to meet with you?"

Jack's heart started racing. "A little bit, but it's always a pleasure to see you, Hayley."

She smiled and began to nervously twist her hair. "You must have noticed that I'm in the shop quite often to buy a coffee?"

"Not overly," replied Jack, lying.

"The truth is, I don't actually like coffee," she continued.

"You drink enough of it," replied Jack.

"I don't. I just throw it away. The truth is I just use the coffee as an excuse to come into your shop."

Jack started to blush and the nervous feeling in his stomach intensified. He took deep breaths to compose himself so he could look surprised at the impending revelation, like an Oscar candidate with a camera focussed on them.

Hayley bowed her head. "This is a little embarrassing, and I know I haven't known you for a while, but the thing is, I really like—"

"I really like you too, Hayley. I think you're amazing," blurted Jack.

"... Emma," continued Hayley. "I really like Emma, Jack," she said. "Oh, no, this just got a little... uncomfortable."

Jack looked blankly, unsure of what had been said and clearly confused. "So, wait, you don't like me?"

Hayley was sensitive to the situation she now found herself in. "No, Jack, you're a lovely person, if a little... quirky, at times. But I'm sorry if I gave you that indication, it wasn't intentional."

"You like Emma? You kept coming into the shop to see Emma, not me?"

"That's correct, Jack, yes. I'm genuinely sorry for the confusion, but I really like Emma."

"But... she's a girl?" said Jack, although he didn't know why. The cogs in his head were working beyond their operational limitations and he began to tap his fingers on the table. "So, why am I here?"

Hayley looked rather sheepish. "I'm thinking I haven't handled this in the best way, but I wanted to ask you if Emma had mentioned me. It's tricky enough trying to meet someone new, especially when you're the same sex as them. She'd been quite affectionate, and I wanted to ask you, as her friend, if she was interested in me? If she was interested in girls?"

"I need another pint," said Jack.

Out of politeness, he motioned to her drink to see if she'd like a refill.

"Yes please, a large glass of house white would be great!"

Later, Jack lay in bed reflecting on the evening. It hadn't been the greatest one; he was out over £100 on the shirt and £30 on drinks, and all to play Cilla Black between Hayley and Emma. One bonus was his confused erection as he thought of the two of them together.

He thought of Emma and grabbed his phone:

> Weird night. Don't speak to Hayley without speaking to me first X

He'd had several pints and the thought of a lie-in was appealing. *Shit,* he thought. *Emma hasn't got a phone.*

"Morning, Derek," said Emma, full of enthusiasm. She hadn't slept well but didn't want her personal life — or lack of one — to impact on her customers further. "You take a seat, my lovely, and I'll bring your tea over in a moment. You're coming to our tea dance at the weekend, Derek?"

His face lit up. "I certainly am, Emma. I've told my daughter that I'm going, and the neighbours. I've got my best bowtie and my suit laid out on the bed."

"Aww, that's lovely," said Emma. "Do you need any help pressing your shirt? There might be a few pretty ladies there!"

Derek giggled. "I hope so! And, no, thank you. I bought a new white shirt and ironed it last night."

Seeing his face and how confident Derek now appeared gave Emma a warm feeling. She was a naturally compassionate person, and so seeing him being pressured into giving money had played heavily on her mind. She'd spoken to a friend at the government who'd promised to raise it and ensure help was available to others in the same situation. She'd also seen a different side to Jack in the last few days. He'd told her about Ray getting ripped off, and a few months ago he'd have laughed it off as some 'old giffer' being stupid enough to give his money away. He still took the piss at how stupid Ray had been, but like Derek with Emma, it played on his mind. It could have easily been his grandad or his mum who'd been conned, and these shit bags cared little about the trail of destruction and devastation they'd left behind. He'd spoken to one of their regulars who worked in a bank about old people being naïve. It was rife, and they had dozens of customers who had fallen victim. The banks were spending a small fortune educating people, so Jack had arranged for a load of brochures to be dropped off at the shop to hand out at the upcoming social events. Jack wasn't heartless but came across as being unconcerned; it was a refreshing change for Emma to see the warmer side of him.

"Morning, Emma," said Hayley, in a soft voice. "You look nice today."

"Oh, you startled me. Thanks, it must be this fetching polo shirt with an overweight Star Wars character on it!"

Hayley looked blankly.

"Jabba the Hutt. It's a play on *Java*." But the vacant glaze didn't change. "Don't worry. One of Jack's bright ideas. How are you? Usual?"

"Yes, please. Is Jack not in?"

"No. Lie-in," said Emma, as she prepared the drink.

"Ah," said Hayley. "Did he by any chance tell you about last night?"

"He did, yes," said Emma, assuming she was talking about the date.

"And... what did you think?"

Emma was a little perplexed. "About last night? I suppose I was a little surprised."

"Surprised in a good way?" pressed Hayley.

"I suppose," said Emma again, slightly confused at the direction the conversation was taking.

Hayley moved closer and placed her hands on the counter. "Could you tell?"

"Erm..." replied Emma, darting her eyes back and forth. "Tell what, exactly?"

Hayley looked around to make sure nobody was in earshot. "You're making me work for this, Emma. Could you tell about my feelings?"

"Ah, okay, sorry. I wasn't sure exactly what you meant. No, I really didn't know you felt that way. When Jack told me, I was surprised as I've usually got a radar for these things. I guess I was totally off on that one."

Hayley looked relieved. "So it hasn't made you uncomfortable? You're okay with it?"

"Of course," said Emma, placing the coffee carefully in front of Hayley. "You only live once, you just have to go with your feelings at times. How does that song go? *Regrets, I've had a few?* You just have to go with it, sometimes." She was hurting inside but determined to show a brave face.

"You're so right, Emma. I can't tell you how pleased that makes me." She moved over to Emma and placed her hands on top of hers. "You're very special," said Hayley, as she leaned in and placed a tender kiss on Emma's lips. Emma stood, rigid, with her nose squashed against Hayley's cheek. Her right eye was partially covered by Hayley's hair, but through the apple-scented locks she could see Derek peering towards them looking somewhat bemused.

Hayley moved back slowly and ran her fingers through her hair, looking for a reaction but none was forthcoming. Emma had lost the power of speech, and her brain was working quicker than her mouth.

"Would you like the coffee to go?" she asked.

Chapter Seven

Welcome to *The Lonely Heart Attack Club*," said Jack, directing people through the coffee shop and towards the stairs at the rear. "Welcome, WELCOME, this way," he said, in a Basil Fawlty-style voice.

Emma punched him on the side of the arm. "Stop calling it that, you spanner, you'll scare them off before they even get in."

Jack ushered two more eager pensioners through the door. "Most of them can't even hear me anyway. I can tell you're still angry."

"Of *course* I'm bloody angry," she replied, through pursed lips. "You had every opportunity to tell Hayley that I'm not into girls."

"How do I know that?" protested Jack.

"My god, are you serious? You've known me all of my adult life and we've worked together for bloody years. At what point during our entire relationship have you gained any insights that I might be attracted to girls?"

"You like the blonde one, from *Game of Thrones*. The dragon lady. You told me so."

"Perspective, Jack. You said that if I was on a shrinking desert island and the only way of escape from shark-infested waters was to sleep with one woman, who would it be? I wouldn't scope her out for a date. *I was about to be eaten by a shark and she was my only escape.*"

Jack shrugged his shoulders. "You still said you would, so I was technically correct that you had shown an interest in girls. Besides, I didn't tell her you were interested in girls, I just didn't tell her that you *weren't*. Anyway, it's not all about you. I'm still hurting because the girl I loved happened to like lady parts more than men parts."

"You didn't tell her because you just wanted the thought of me and Hayley together, didn't you?"

"Little bit, yes. If I wasn't going to see her naked, I was hoping you would, so you could tell me what she looked like."

"You're such a loser!" said Emma. "So if I asked you if you were on a desert island—"

"Hugh Grant."

"Crikey, you didn't have to think about that, Jack."

"What's to think about? Hugh Grant all day long, loveable cheeky chap, what's not to like. I'd totally get it on with Hugh," said Jack.

Two portly, elderly ladies approached, and Jack greeted them with a beaming smile. "Excuse me, ladies, does your mum know you're out this late?"

The lady to the left started to giggle and leaned in towards her friend to explain the joke. "Flattery will get you everywhere," she chuckled. "Everywhere," she repeated, much to Jack's unease.

"It's a great turnout," said Emma. "We must have about thirty people in by now, I hope Pete is looking after them."

The two older ladies, who were dressed almost identically, doubled back on themselves and Jack took a defensive position behind Emma. "Excuse me," said one of them. "Where's the bingo?"

Emma looked puzzled. "It's not bingo, my love, it's a social club for the older people in the community. You're very welcome to come and socialise?"

"Oh," she responded. "We just got off the bus and followed the rest of them. We thought it was bingo."

They talked amongst themselves for a moment before shuffling upstairs. "What a lovely idea, we'd love to stay. Be sure to send your friend up later," said the one with slightly better hearing.

Emma laughed. "No problem, I'll have him washed and sent upstairs for you!"

A very attractive brunette approached the shop, clearly unsure where she was going. She stuck her nose to the glass and peered inside. Jack pointed towards the door and moved eagerly to greet her. "Can I help?"

She reached inside her considerable briefcase and pulled out a folded piece of paper. "Sorry, I'm a bit out of breath, I've already been to two wrong places. Is this, *The Lonely Heart Attack Club?*" she asked.

Emma was about to protest the name, but it did have a certain ring to it. "Yes, well, upstairs is. How can we help?"

"Great! I'm Shelby Sullivan from Manx Radio. We've had a few calls from people telling us what you're doing down here, and we'd love to get an interview, if that's okay with you?"

Emma was a little nervous and pushed Jack towards her. "Of course, he'd love to. Can I get you a drink?"

"Water would be fantastic, thank you. Yes, we've had a number of people getting in touch and telling us what a fantastic initiative you're working on. I must apologise, I didn't know where you were, but I'll be sure to let people know. What does 'Ava the Hutt' mean?"

"It's *Java,* actually," explained Jack. "But the 'J' fell off and I haven't had it replaced," he said, a little embarrassed

"Ah, I see. As in Jabba the Hutt. I like it. Anyway, it won't be a live interview, so if you make a mistake we can just go over again, right?" She took a small digital recorder with an unfeasibly large microphone and pushed it towards his face. "Are you ready? Great."

Shelby: I'm in the heart of Douglas with Jack, the owner of the popular coffee shop, Java the Hutt. Jack, aside from selling delicious coffee — which I've still not had [laughing] — I hear you've started a new initiative. Please, do tell us more.

Jack: Hi Shelby, you'd be welcome for a coffee anytime [more laughing, followed by awkward pause]. I was very aware that a lot of my client base was elderly... [sees Emma glaring in background and corrects] ... well, along with my friend and business partner, Emma [points nervously]. And we heard some harrowing tales about people — particularly elderly — being manipulated and falling victim to some fairly sophisticated scams.

Shelby: How awful. Can you give me an example?

Jack: Yes, a friend of ours gave a donation to charity. It was nothing excessive, but as much as he could afford. But, before long, he was being tortured by dozens of them pressurising him for money. What started off as a good intention nearly finished him off. Another friend of ours ended up getting taken in by a couple of sexy-sounding American sisters, who sold him a load of shares in companies that didn't exist.

Shelby: And what amounts of money did they lose?

Jack: Tens of thousands. We heard that it's happened to a number of people in the Isle of Man.

Shelby: And it's a social club and, dare I say it, a dating club on occasion? I believe you've coined the phrase *The Lonely Heart Attack Club?*

Jack: It's not the official title, Shelby. First and foremost, though, it's a social club. It's a known fact that large portions of our elderly population are simply lonely.

More and more social clubs have had funding reduced and people are sat alone in their house all day. It's probably why they're happy to speak to the fraudsters because no other bugger is phoning them. We wanted to set up a social club and also use it as a platform to educate people about the types of fraud that are out there, and also introduce them to technology which will help them keep in touch with distant friends and family — such as Facebook and FaceTime. Also, at the end of the day, we're also a small business struggling to compete against the big corporates. Anything we can do to bring people into the shop will really help us, so this is a win-win for all concerned.

Shelby: It sounds fantastic, Jack. It really is impressive and hopefully you can help older people extend their social network and drum up some much-needed business. So, what do you have planned in the social club?

Jack: [now clueless] Well, we've got a bit of a dance going on upstairs today. If that does well, we'll maybe do that once a month. We were thinking of doing a speed dating event, maybe a day trip outing if we get enough interest. We just want to do something to get the word out there and raise awareness. What do you think we could do?

Shelby: Hold on, *I'm* supposed to be interviewing *you*. Okay, something different to raise awareness, hmmm, what about doing a sponsored run? Or, what about setting a world record? [laughs]

Jack: [Uncomfortable silence] Great idea, Shelby. We'll set a world record.

Shelby: Well, folks, you heard it here first. A world record attempt, no less. So if you'd like to know more, people can pop into the shop [Jack nods] and have a coffee with Jack and Emma.

"And, that's us finished, Jack. Well done," said Shelby, packing her bag. "Sorry I can't stop, but I will come back for that coffee, soon! Thanks again, and I hope the guys upstairs have fun. Bye, Emma."

Emma waved, and Jack could tell by her body language that all was not well in the zoo. "A world record, seriously?" she said. "What on earth were you thinking, telling her we were going to enter a world record like that?"

Jack chewed his lip and stroked his chin. "Yeah, it was a bit left-field. I'm not entirely sure where that one came from. The conversation went a bit quiet and I just panicked, I suppose. I get nervous with silence, and I'm not good at saying nothing."

He knew instantly that he'd said something wrong. Emma appeared to double her mass, and was drawn up, almost on tiptoe. "You're not good at saying nothing? You have to be taking the piss. You were perfectly fine to say nothing when Hayley wanted to know if I liked girls. You were quite the master at keeping that big, ginormous pie-hole quiet when that vital bit of clarity was required."

He smiled; he had to give her that. "Yeah, fair point. Anyway, buddy, pal, business partner, think of the PR if we get a load of old people working together in a world record. We can even promote the other stuff, the scams and all that. We can't lose. If we fail, everyone will think it's the old people, how cute, and all that. Winner-winner-chicken-dinner."

Emma shrank back to normal size and placed her feet firmly back on the ground. "You know what, Jack, for an ill-conceived irrational comment, it's actually pretty good. We'd be helping people, getting business into the shop, and also spreading awareness amongst the vulnerable in the community. If you'd told me about this as a well-thought-out idea, I'd think it was genius. As it happens, you just got lucky. Come on, let's go and see how Pete is getting on..."

"It looks fabulous!" said Emma, leaning into Jack.

"What?" said Jack, unable to hear over the sound of "Agadoo" by Black Lace. "I can't hear you? The room looks great though, doesn't it?"

The neighbouring shops knew about the event and were fully supportive. With their help and assistance, they'd turned the upstairs of the coffee shop into a mini disco, with flashing lights, disco ball, and a full sound system. There had been a steady stream of food dropped in during the day and several tables were full of refreshments. DJ Pete was masterful in charge of the music and encouraging the ageing audience to their feet. He was dressed in a green Lycra catsuit which left nothing to the imagination and sported a pair of flashing green baubles that attached to springs on his head.

Emma felt a little like a teacher presiding over a school disco as she walked around waving at the guests. She indicated to Pete to lower the volume as she didn't want to damage what little hearing some of the revellers had.

"It was a bit strange at first," said Pete. "The boys were sat on one side, and the girls on the other, just staring at each other in a cute, wrinkly kind of way. Those two, over there, got on the dance floor when I put a bit of Rick Astley on and haven't sat down since. As soon as they got up, they dragged some of the others up and they love it now."

Emma laughed and prodded Jack. "It's the two bingo girls. Looks like they got the party started. I'll be sure to send them your way later, Jack."

"I think they're pissed," said Pete. "The one on the right — with the lighter shade of orange hair — keeps pulling out a hipflask. Fair play to them!"

Emma took Jack by the hand and dragged him onto the dance floor. "Bet you wish I was Hugh Grant! We've done well here, Jack. Look around, there must be twenty, twenty-five, thirty people here, that would ordinarily be sat at home with the TV for company. We can make a real difference."

Jack nodded. "Yup, it's quite a nice feeling doing something nice. And it looks like I won't need my mop after all, which is a bonus."

He felt a tap on the shoulder. "Do you mind if I cut in?" asked Derek. "Although I'm sure this young lady has a very full dance card."

Jack obliged and headed to the refreshment tables, taking care to give the drunken bingo ladies a wide berth.

"You look very handsome, Derek."

"Thank you, Emma. It's been a long while since I had cause to wear a suit and I've thoroughly enjoyed it. I met someone tonight that I've not seen for twenty years and it turns out he lives less than ten minutes away from me, it's remarkable. I do hope you look to do another one of these events as everyone looks like they're having a good time."

"We will, most definitely. We're looking into maybe doing a day trip out somewhere nice if people are interested. Has your daughter been calling you on the new number?"

"Oh, yes. It's wonderful. I apologised that I hadn't been answering the calls. Now I look back I realise how daft I'd been."

"It's not daft, Derek. It's easily done, and the important thing is that we've sorted it for you. Next, we'll get you set up on FaceTime so you can see those lovely grandchildren."

Derek's eyes lit up. "That would be wonderful. My daughter is having the children christened in a couple of months."

"That's lovely, are you going to go?" asked Emma, but she could tell by his expression that he was apprehensive.

"I'm not sure. At my age, heading off on an adventure might be a bit too much."

"Derek," she said, in a firm but friendly tone, "I thought we were friends. What's really up?"

He smiled. "We are friends, best of friends. It's a bit more expensive to get to Italy than I thought. I have some money but I wanted to keep that for special occasions to buy the children presents. Unfortunately, those charity people have taken most of the money I was keeping to one side."

"Would your daughter help?"

"I dare say she would, Emma. But I'm a stubborn old so-and-so, and if it meant borrowing off her, then I wouldn't want to go. Anyway, enough of my troubles, I don't want to put a downer on this wonderful evening and it's not often I get to waltz with such a beautiful young lady."

"I'll need to be careful," said Emma. "The other women are giving me an evil look for dancing with the most handsome man in here."

The refreshment table was soon decimated, and Emma made sure that everyone had a 'doggy bag' to go home with. They took the scam brochures received from the bank and placed one in each bag. The guests were a little unsure how to take Pete but soon warmed to him, with most insisting on a dance with the green goddess.

"Your grandad looks a little comfortable with the bingo girls, Jack. Do you think you should go and rescue him?"

"No chance. He's big enough and ugly enough to look after himself. Besides, after Randy Sandy, I doubt those two will scare him. He probably thinks he's on for a threesome, how does it go, two fat ladies — eighty-eight!"

"Eww, nice thought," replied Emma, making a face. "Hmm, I noticed Hayley didn't come with her gran," she said, changing subject. "I hope I haven't upset her, as I really like her. As a friend and neighbour, I mean."

Jack looked inquisitive. "Yeah, but wouldn't you just..."

"No," Emma replied, "I wouldn't. Draw a line under it and move on. I think I handled it fairly well with her, aside from the initial shock. I'll leave it a couple of days and if I don't see her, I'll pop in and say hello. I don't want things to get awkward."

"Great night!" said Geoffrey. "Truly, I really enjoyed it."

"Thanks, Grandad. Are you okay to get home?"

He had sweat dripping down his forehead from all the dancing and a vague red lipstick outline on his cheek. "Going home?" he said. "I'm going into town for a couple of drinks with these two!" The two bingo girls grabbed one of his arms each and escorted him down the stairs.

Emma sat in the coffee shop with her feet on the table and her hands supporting the back of her head. It was just after ten p.m., and for the first time, she could relax. The social club hadn't been a chore, but she'd wanted it to go well so had little time to relax. The shop was empty and cleaned down for the next morning; she smiled as she reached for a cold bottle of cider, chilled to toast the evening. The street was busy with people enjoying the weekend; some a little too much, as an unsteady girl wearing next to nothing fell into the doorway of the shop. Much to the amusement of her friends she struggled to steady herself, but they soon moved safely on their way. Emma often felt old before her time, and pondered on whether she should be the one moving uneasily through the town centre wearing next to nothing. It wasn't that she didn't enjoy going out — she did — but the thought of spending a fortune on a night out and dying the following day in bed didn't appeal. She often reflected on whether she was boring or just sensible. But, as she dwelled on the evening she realised that her motivation was in making other people happy. She thought of Derek and the other people who'd come to their social club and how what they were doing was making a difference. They hadn't discovered a cure for cancer or promoted world peace, but they were making a small but significant impact on the people in their community. She smiled as she thought of Derek in his finest suit and how happy he'd been as he twirled her around the dance floor. Only a few short weeks before, Derek was at a low point in his life that nearly ended it. Emma reflected on the girls enjoying themselves and where she was and knew she wouldn't change anything for the world; she felt contented.

Her moment of contemplation was broken as Jack pushed the door open. "I've bought us chips."

"We've got a fridge full of sandwiches," said Emma. "But, mmm, they do smell good. Thank you for walking Derek home. I know he'd be fine, but with it being the weekend."

"You don't need to explain. I like the old boy. He was just telling me about his time in the merchant navy. He is a very interesting man and I get the impression he was quite a character in his youth. He told me he once boxed at Madison Square Garden."

"Did he win?" asked Emma, as she passed a bottle of cider across the table.

"We didn't get to that, but I got the impression that the result was less important than the experience. Cheers!" said Jack, before taking an appreciative mouthful of cider. "I enjoyed today. I'll be honest, I didn't think I would. I thought you were a bit mental even suggesting it, but it's brought punters in the shop and it was good to see them enjoying themselves tonight. You've done well!"

"What are you smiling at?" asked Emma.

Jack paused for a moment, in his own thoughts. "How the hell are we going to break a world record?"

"Well, it's out there now. The entire Island knows about it," said Emma.

"I think you're being a bit generous to their listening figures, but we'll think of something. We could juggle old people or have the world's oldest conga line. We should be inundated with oldies after tonight's festivities, especially if the boys hear about the bingo girls!"

Emma replaced the empty bottles and leaned closer to Jack. "I think there is a softer side in there, you know. You can come across as a bit of a…"

"Dickhead?"

"No. Well, okay, sometimes. You give the impression that you don't take anything serious. A bit of a loveable buffoon."

Jack looked a little hurt. "So, you're saying I'm a bit of a feckless wonder?"

"You can appear as someone that only cares about Jack — which I know isn't true — but it's nice that other people get to see what you're really like."

Jack moved even closer. "Oh, and what am I really like?"

"Stupid. Funny and caring… when you want to be, that is. Jack, I'm really sorry it didn't go as expected with Hayley. I know you really liked her," said Emma, placing a hand on top of his.

"Ah, what are you going to do? At least I lost out to someone who is 'smoking' hot."

It may have been the bottle and a half of cider, but Emma moved her head closer to Jack. His eyes widened and the grip on his hand intensified. He closed his eyes in anticipation. He could smell her perfume and feel her breath as she moved nearer.

"Jack," whispered Emma. "Jack, I think your grandad is half-naked, leaning against the window."

"What! Aww, what's that stupid old bugger up to now? He's going to get himself arrested, again."

Emma put a hand over her face to stifle a laugh, but the appearance of someone his age dancing in his underwear was a bit too much to take.

Geoffrey noticed Emma and waved enthusiastically. "I've been drinking Jägerbombs," he said, slurring his words.

Jack tried frantically to cover him with a tablecloth, but his gyrating made it difficult. "Emma, can you lock up? I need to get him dressed and home before he gets locked up!"

"Sure. No problem, go!"

She continued laughing as Jack fought to cover his grandad with the white tablecloth. "He looks like a drunken ghost!" shouted Emma, through the street — which was fortunately deserted.

Emma could hear the sound of Geoffrey singing, long after he'd moved out of visual range. She returned inside and placed her feet back on the table. She took her bottle of cider and ran her finger around the top. Her head tilted back as she thought of Jack and the mere image brought a smile to her face and made her cheeks flush.

She took Jack's bottle and knocked it against her own. "Cheers! Here's to Jack and Emma," she said, with a hint of optimism in her voice.

Chapter Eight

The perimeter tables of the coffee shop had been positioned to form one long imposing table in the middle of the room. It was covered with tablecloths that were differing shades of white, depending on their age. Three water jugs were placed in the centre and twelve glasses sat in front of each of the invited audience. The scene was like an outtake from a budget version of *The Sopranos*. Five older men — including Ray, Geoffrey, and Derek — sat on one side, and five women — including Hayley, her gran, and the Bingo Girls — on the other. Emma sat with her back to the front window, at the head of the table, and Jack sat at the opposite end.

"Order, order!" said Jack, who appeared to be enjoying his position as meeting chair. His instruction was ignored as the muffled chatter continued. "Hayley, give them two a nudge, will you, and tell them to turn them up?" he said, mimicking adjustment of volume control on a hearing aid.

"I know it's teatime," he continued. "And I know you have busy lives. Well, that's a lie, as most of you would be at home watching the grass grow. But thanks for coming to The Lonely Heart Attack committee meeting. You've all had two weeks to think about our world record attempt, so we either need to come up with something or we need to bow out in disgrace and end our lives in mediocracy."

Emma shook her head. "Inspirational, Mr Chairman, truly inspiring."

One of the Bingo Girls leaned closer to her friend. "What did he say?" but her attempt at a whisper was only a fraction of a decibel below normal talking voice.

"Record attempt," repeated Jack, a little slower and louder.

She smiled and nodded her head. "Coffee would be wonderful, James."

Jack turned around to see if they'd been joined by a new barista that he hadn't been introduced to. Slightly perturbed, he continued. "Okay, let's go 'round the table. Grandad, why don't you start us off?"

Geoffrey cleared his throat and placed a pair of thin-rimmed glasses over his nose. He reached inside the pocket of his navy-blue blazer and with purpose, slowly pulled out a neatly folded piece of paper. He gave a knowing wink to the bingo girls sat opposite which drew a flirtatious giggle.

"With the help of my wonderful grandson, Jack, I've been perusing the joys of the internet. In particular, for inspiration about world records."

"That wasn't all, Grandad, was it?" interrupted Jack.

The Bingo Girls looked a little traumatized. "Oh, you heard that just fine!" replied Geoffrey. "Anyway, my research has uncovered that one thousand and ten bikini-clad women posed on an Australian beach, setting a record for the world's largest swimsuit photo."

Jack looked impressed as his eyes fell upon Hayley and Emma. Emma smiled and pointed towards the older ladies surrounding the table which brought him back to earth like a cold shower. Sensing that the committee were not bought in, he flipped his piece of paper to the other side. "This one sounds fun. In twenty-fourteen, four hundred and six people set a record for simultaneous twerking. I'm not entirely sure what twerking is, but I can show you what they were doing."

Jack placed a gentle but firm hand on his shoulder, pushing him back into his seat. "Thanks, Grandad, I'm sure we can use our imaginations."

The evening drew painfully on and due to their collective ages, toilet breaks were a constant interruption. The frustration was evident in Jack's voice as one stupid idea after another was motioned and quickly vetoed. Even Emma, who was fairly rational, provided little in the way of sensible input, including one idea involving a pogo stick and another to do with a watermelon and a domestic cat. Jack groaned in frustration, but as Emma quickly pointed out, he'd brought nothing of merit to the table.

Jack looked at Hayley, who was as radiant as ever. Even though he knew he had a snowball in hell's chance of anything romantic, his heart still fluttered whenever he saw her. She'd been somewhat distant over the last few days, so he was delighted that she'd agreed to attend. There was no cause to, of course, but Hayley had felt uneasy and ultimately a little bit humiliated — similar to the way Jack had come away from the whole affair. Hayley's gran sat on her left side, and exuded elegance by the way she dressed and carried herself; although she was into her seventies, Jack had still thrown several curious glances her way, as had the more mature gentlemen in the room.

"Hayley, a pleasure to have you with us. Are you going to save us with the glimmer of a sensible suggestion?" asked Jack.

Hayley blushed a little as the attention turned to her. "I'm not sure about that. Gran and I were thinking about this, and wondered perhaps whether we could do something gardening-related?"

"Mmm, yes," said Jack. "The idea is growing on me…" He waited for the expected laugh in appreciation of his pun, but it wasn't forthcoming. "What are you thinking?"

"There were a couple," continued Hayley. "One was the world's largest hanging basket," she said, which evoked a murmured mumble in the room. "The other was the world's largest horizontal wall of flowers."

"Oh, I like that!" said Emma. "That sounds like great fun."

Hayley showed the room an image of the giant flower wall on her iPad. "A seed company in Suffolk holds the current record. It's a wall of flowers over two hundred feet long with more than twenty thousand blooms. Isn't it stunning!"

Even Jack was enthused by the suggestion, moving in for a closer look. "That's a great idea, Hayley."

She smiled. "We thought it was a project that the community could get involved in. It would be a lot of work but I'm sure we'd have enough people to get involved."

"That's a lot of flowers," said Emma. "It'll cost a fortune to get enough?"

Hayley nodded. "It will, but we wondered whether we could get some sponsorship and maybe some help from the government. If you think about it, we'd be creating a project that hundreds of people could get involved with, so it'd be great for a sponsorship opportunity, also, it'd be a bit of a tourist attraction for the town. We could use it to promote local business — such as ours — and also the work we're trying to do in educating the vulnerable in our community. We could maybe sell small bunches of flowers and people could put a dedication to their loved ones. We could donate the proceeds to charity, maybe scam victims?"

Derek cleared his throat. "I think it's a wonderful idea, truly, wonderful. If you let me, I'd be honoured to get involved. I don't have much money, but I do have a lot of spare time I can give."

Emma smiled at Derek. "I think it's a wonderful idea, also. We could ask Shelby to put something on the radio to advertise it."

"I'd be happy to arrange that!" said Jack.

"If we're trying to help older people not get ripped off, we should try and spread the message further than the Isle of Man," said Geoffrey.

"We could set up a live webcam," said Emma.

"I like where you're going with this," replied Jack enthusiastically. "I'd be happy to help with that, also. We could do with getting someone famous involved, and I think I know just the person." His gaze moved slowly to Hayley, who looked bemused. She took a moment, then shrugged her shoulders.

"Kelvin Reed!" said Jack. "He'd be ideal."

Geoffrey struggled with the name for a moment. "Is he not the chap on the TV? The gardener? Didn't he go to jail or something?"

"No," said Hayley, slightly offended. "He had a few issues with his, *ahem…* socialising. As a result, he's not on the television as much as he once was."

"Oh, yes, I forgot about that. Dogging, wasn't it? We could get him on the cheap, then?" asked Jack.

"Gran is closer to that side of the family, but I'm sure we could look into it," said Hayley.

"Great, I think we have a bit of a plan. Trump was going to build a wall, but ours is going to be much better, I think. With that, are there any final questions before we adjourn?"

Derek slowly raised his right arm and gently raised a finger like an inquisitive schoolboy. "Excuse me, Jack. What does *dogging* mean?"

Postman Pete leaned over the counter and motioned Emma. "Is he okay?" he asked. Jack cut a solitary figure sat near the window with his head embedded in a pile of paperwork. He didn't even lift his head as Pete flounced in on his morning rounds. Jack had the attention span of a three-year-old and to see him reviewing paperwork was unique.

"He's fine. He's been on to the Guinness World Record people and they've given him some paperwork and rules he needs to work through."

"I'm suitably impressed. He's taking this seriously, then?" asked Pete.

"Totally, it's great to see. It has gone a bit crazy over the last few days. But in a good way, as people want to get involved. The bank who gave us the brochures want to give us some sponsorship money, and the Douglas Town Hall has pretty much given us carte blanche, subject to applying for a permit. They've even said we can build the wall in the Sunken Gardens!"

Pete caught her off guard. "And… what about you two?"

Emma blushed, and tried to divert the conversation without success.

Pete was persistent. "C'mon, Emma. Spill!"

She dropped the tea towel on the countertop and took her head into her hands. "Aww, Pete, I don't know what to do."

"Darling, you're absolutely stunning, you could have your pick of any man. Are you sure you want Jack to be that man?"

She looked a little coy. "I don't know. We had a moment the other night. We nearly kissed."

Pete instantly moved closer; his attention and focus were now directed completely at Emma. He thrived on gossip. He became giddy at the prospect; it was an insatiable thirst to him, much like the blood of a fresh virgin was to a vampire. Emma knew this and was careful how much information she wanted to divulge. If she'd told him about the advances of Hayley, he'd have had a gossip overload and likely imploded. "Go on," he said.

"That's it. We nearly kissed, but we were interrupted by the partially-covered arse cheeks of his grandad," replied Emma. "In fact… Jack!" she shouted, "I can still see the outline of Grandad's bum cheeks on the window! You said you were going to give it a wash!"

"I'm not going near his arse!" replied Jack, without turning.

"Not Grandad, the windows!"

Pete was eager to get her back to the matter in hand. "So, what are you going to do?"

"Well, I've told him that I'm going to come around to his flat and cook him a nice meal, as a reward for all of the good work he's been doing, and we'll see what happens. I don't know why I like him. If you'd told me six months ago, I'd have said you were mental. I mean, look at him. He's got a pencil poking out of his ear."

"Why?" asked Pete.

"It kept rolling off the table and he figured it was the best place to keep it for easy access. This is what I'm on about. He's a complete tool. But he's, well... he's Jack."

"You don't have to tell me, Emma. If he wasn't straight, I'd definitely be giving him a special delivery."

Jack walked over to them and was a little suspicious of the smirks that greeted him. "Hey, Pete. What's up?"

"Nothing, I was just talking to Emma about your post box."

"I'm not asking," said Jack. "Do you want to know the good news, Emma?"

"It would make a nice change, please do!"

"Well, I've been looking over the accounts."

Emma was flabbergasted. "Seriously? I thought you were looking over the record stuff or dirty magazines. Okay, but can you take the pencil out first?" she asked.

Jack took the pencil from his ear and to the disgust of Emma, placed it in his mouth. He took the paperwork he'd been working on, which had a series of arbitrary scribbles on them. "We've been quite busy in here over the last few weeks and the good news is that we can now pay the overdue rent to Jasmine, which means we're not going to get chucked out on our arse!"

"Excellent," said Emma. "Does that mean we can pay ourselves something?"

He looked back at his paperwork and tapped the pencil on his calculator for a moment. "Well... soon. The rent is up-to-date, so a few more days like this and we should be able to sort ourselves out."

Emma looked relieved. "That's good, my savings account is emptier than a... than a... Oh, I'm shit at those. I always think of a great example the next day, when the moment's gone."

The three of them proceeded to look vacantly at each other. "Emptier than a hermit's address book?" offered Pete. "Okay, on that, I'm going. Love to all."

Emma looked quizzically at Jack. "You're still smiling. You looked contented."

"And that's bad?"

"No, not at all. It's good!"

"I'm just glad that things seem to be on the up. I'm fed up just surviving, and sometimes not even that. I hate it that you do all of this work and don't even take a wage. I do appreciate you, Emma."

Emma punched him playfully on the arm. "Don't be a big blouse, I'm not used to seeing you being grateful. Can I help with this record attempt?"

"No," he shrugged. "It's on track. I'm just not sure about bringing Kelvin over. Hayley said he's happy to come but we'll need to give him five hundred pounds."

Emma scowled. "Tell him to do one, then?"

Jack paused. "I know, that was my first reaction. If we want to get the message out, further than the Isle of Man, then he is quite well-known. He will drag a few of the oldies in as well, as they love him. We've got a few quid coming in as sponsorship, so the money is there to bring him over. I suppose the question is, do we want to put on a low-scale event, or try and raise the profile to a wider audience?"

"He's a bit of a deviant, isn't he?" asked Emma.

Jack paused again. "Well who isn't? Besides, as Derek confirmed, the oldies don't even know what dogging is. They'll probably think it's something to do with Crufts."

"I'm not entirely sure what it is, either?" admitted Emma. "I mean, I think I get the general idea."

"You don't know what dogging is?"

Emma looked offended. "Why would I possibly have a clear understanding of what dogging is? It's not exactly something that comes up in sex education classes at school, and, if you're in a normal relationship, I suspect the offer of dogging is not usually on the agenda. Anyway, how are you such an authority on dogging? Are you in the club? Are you a *dogger?*"

"Let's just say I was an inquisitive teenager and I had the internet."

Emma looked revolted. "Eww, I'm not sure I want to cook you dinner anymore!"

"Cooking? I think the shop can stretch to a night out for us on Saturday, steak and a nice bottle of vino. I can bring you up to speed with the world of dogging. And, on that subject, I think I'll get Kelvin booked in to come over. I'm looking forward to this, we could be world record holders this time next month."

Emma rubbed his shoulder affectionately. "How many have you got signed up for your 'Silver Sprinters'?"

Jack took the notepad from next to the phone and thumbed through the pages. "Seven!" he announced proudly. "You should come, I'm only taking them for a run across the promenade. Or, well, a brisk stroll."

"Check you out! A few months ago you'd have been out of breath opening a tin of beans, and you're now running an exercise class."

"I know! Even Ray signed up, so hopefully he'll put in an appearance."

"Great," said Emma. "He could do with shifting a few pounds. Hopefully he's off the drink, I couldn't smell any on him when he's been in. As much as I'd love to join you all, I've got a date with a hot bath and a good book."

A firm breeze whipped through the Douglas seafront; you could taste the salt spray off the Irish Sea in the air. The vast promenade stood empty apart from resilient joggers and a cyclist harassed by the swirling winds. Running parallel to the promenade were several sunken gardens. Accessed by descending steps at each end, there were a series of floral gardens crowned by an ornate fountain, designed in Victorian times when the Isle of Man was a destination of choice for the discerning tourist. The visitors still came — albeit in smaller numbers — and on a more clement day the gardens would be filled with people enjoying a sea breeze or perhaps workers taking their lunch break. Jack stood on the promenade and peered over the wall into the Sunken Gardens. Here, in a few short weeks, would be a wall of flowers long enough to get them into the Guinness Book of World Records.

How the hell did I get involved in this? he thought.

He turned towards the sea, performing a series of deep lunges. He cracked his fingers and walked up the line of people who spanned the width of the promenade.

"I don't like you and I don't care what you think about me," he barked, in a fairly aggressive tone. He held his steely expression as he walked up the line with his lip snarled like a bad Elvis impersonator.

"What is it?" he shouted, as Derek raised his hand.

He looked almost apologetic. "Jack, I like you. I'm sure we all do. If we've upset you, should we go?"

"No, no, it's fine. Sorry, Derek. I was just trying to motivate you all, you know, like one of those drill sergeants in American war films? There were a series of confused-looking faces. "Okay, I'll leave the motivational speech and we'll just get on? That's where we're going," said Jack, pointing towards the end of the promenade. "Just over two miles, each way, is everyone in?" Jack jogged down the line and offered a high-five to the assembled ranks. Everyone was quick to respond except for a diminutive white-haired lady in a pink tracksuit who hovered a pace or two behind everyone else. "Don't be shy!" said Jack, taking her by the hand. "We're all friends here, what's your name?"

"Dorothy," she replied. "It's just that..."

"C'mon, Dorothy, you're now a Silver Sprinter!" And with that, Jack ushered the group — which now numbered nine — into a brisk pace along the promenade. He moved to the rear of the group to encourage the momentum. "That's it, Dorothy, you're going well!"

With the assistance of Jack, his grandad had reviewed his exercise attire. He sported a pair of brilliant white pumps and had a matching blue short/vest combo which from a distance made him look like a deflated American wrestler. He was eager, and despite the headwind pushed on with vigour. Derek was a little more delicate as he shuffled in his smart brown slacks with a brown wind keeper jacket. He was determined and had a huge beaming smile as he wiped the remnants of salty water from his cheeks.

"You're looking well, Ray. How're you feeling?" asked Jack, moving alongside.

His eyes were not as set back, and his huge nose was now almost skin tone rather than an unhealthy red glow. "I've not touched a drop for two weeks, son. I'm feeling good. A few more of these walks and I'll get rid of this gut," he said, placing his hands on his stomach like an expectant mother.

Jack took the opportunity to recruit the Silver Sprinters to his world record and they were all delighted to get involved. He wasn't convinced that a couple of them knew what he was on about, but they seemed eager enough.

The promenade was curved like a half-moon, and as they progressed to the one-mile mark the slight change in direction saw them move out of the direct wind and into welcome shelter. Their ears and cheeks were tingling and as the wind subsided Jack could hear a faint shouting. He ignored it at first, but it became louder. He turned and performed a quick roll call, in case someone had fallen. *No man left behind,* he thought.

All were present and accounted for, but as he turned completely out of the wind his hearing became more attuned. The promenade was virtually empty, so it wasn't difficult to isolate where the shouting was emanating from. Jack walked backwards, keeping pace with the group. A frail man in a wheelchair was turning his wheels at pace. He was clearly not dressed for the weather in a thin white short-sleeved shirt that offered no protection from the elements. Jack slowed as the man was clearly distressed and as he closed in, Jack could see he only had one leg. His thinning white hair moved erratically, and Jack was impressed at the pace he was able to extract from the chair.

"Are you okay there?" asked Jack, but it was clear from the expression that the man was furious.

He had a wooden curved walking stick attached to the rear of the chair and when he was three or four meters from Jack, he released one hand and took the stick firmly in his right hand. He held the stick aloft and continued to turn the wheel at a rapid pace with his left hand; he looked like a valiant knight preparing to slay a formidable dragon. Jack didn't know which direction to move and fearing a collision he took a step back, but as he did the rubber grip at the bottom of the walking stick caught him directly on the left testicle. He barked in pain as the wind flew out of his lungs and the agony struck him like a sledgehammer. He fell to the floor and took up a foetal position, gently covering his groin.

"You bloody pervert!" shouted the wheeled aggressor, who continued to wave his stick menacingly.

Jack whimpered until the pain subsided and as he looked up, the Silver Sprinters had formed a circle and were looking down on him. Despite the pain, he was intrigued at how different they all looked as their loose skin dangled in the wind.

"What have you done now?" asked Grandad.

Jack pushed himself to a seated position. "Nothing, I don't think? Professor Xavier just attacked me for no reason, and why do people keep calling me a pervert lately? It hurts!"

The man held the stick close to Jack's face. "Done nothing? You call kidnap nothing? What is this, anyway?" he asked, looking at the congregated group. "Are you the leader of some cult for old people?"

Dorothy stepped forward and piloted the stick away from Jack's face. "Okay, Thomas, put the stick down."

"I've been chasing you bloody idiots for the last mile!" he shouted. "Give me my Dorothy back, or I'll push this stick so far up your arse it'll knock your teeth out!"

"Dorothy, anytime you want to step in would be appreciated," said Jack, with a nervous laugh.

"I did try to tell you," she said, taking refuge behind the wheelchair. "We were going for a coffee and forgot his coat. As I walked back to the car, you grabbed me."

"You're a pervert!" shouted Thomas.

Jack began to protest and as he looked for allies, his grandad folded his arms and shook his head. "Should be locked up for grabbing women off the street!" he said.

"Grandad... Jesus! There are a time and a place for your humour, and this isn't it. Dorothy, why did you follow us for the last twenty-five minutes?" asked Jack, in disbelief.

She was becoming rather overwhelmed. "Well, you all seemed to know me, and I didn't have chance to protest. The lady next to me hasn't stopped talking about her varicose veins and weak bladder since we set off."

Jack raised his hands like he was preaching to his disciples. "Look, there has clearly been an innocent mistake. Let's move on. You're both welcome to join us for the return leg, but to be clear, it's not a cult and I'm not a pervert. We're the Silver Sprinters."

Their new guests needed to follow the route back, so cautiously agreed to the invitation. Thomas kept a gentle grip of his stick, ready to unleash it at a moment's notice — a point that hadn't gone unnoticed by Jack, who walked like he'd just dismounted a horse. As they commenced on the return leg, their numbers began to swell — much like Jack's left testicle. Other mature walkers joined the group and by the time they approached the final stretch, there were fifteen people enjoying an evening walk. Jack stood proudly at the head of the group and as he turned to look at the determined faces, he felt like Rocky Balboa on a training run through the Philadelphia streets.

He was unsure how the idea would be taken, but all things considered, the night had been a huge success. Not only was it getting people to exercise, but he was giving people of a certain age the opportunity to socialise with people from the same generation. He'd always taken companionship for granted, but he now understood how important it truly was, and how destructive not having it could be. Grandad, Derek, and the others chatted like old friends and were busy making arrangements for the next meeting and Jack had recruited further numbers for his record attempt. He listened in on Ray who repeated his experiences with Candy and Charity, and if people were not too embarrassed to share their experiences then, hopefully, it would prevent others from falling victim to the same scam.

Jack collapsed into bed; tired, but with a genuine sense of contentment. He was enjoying being selfless. As he reflected on it, he realised how he'd often been selfish. Bizarrely he was getting more fulfilment being selfless than selfish, which he thought a strange irony.

He picked up his phone and eagerly texted Emma:

> Great night. Got 15 volunteers to help us with the w/record. Got assaulted by one-legged OAP in wheelchair. Not sure if I can have kids anymore. X

As he drifted off to sleep he felt good, better than he'd done for a long time. There were aspects of his life he'd been unclear on, and as he thought about where he was taking Emma for a meal, he sat bolt upright. She'd been great lately, and he didn't like it if he was apart from her for too long. Until now he'd passed it off as them being good friends. He didn't know whether it was the exercise or the fresh sea air, but he had an overwhelming moment of clarity.

Shit! he thought. *I'm in love with Emma?*

Chapter Nine

The Northern Line Tube was stifling and overcrowded. The peak of the rush hour was in full flow, with hordes of people scurrying like ants through the network of tunnels. The motion of the train caused a suave thirty-something man to deviate momentarily from his constricted territory. He composed himself, and as he reclaimed his position he turned to apologise for imposing himself. He had an impressive head of styled, jet-black hair and his suit exuded class; he was clearly a man of influence. He pinched the knot of his tie and feigned an apologetic grin as he leaned towards the demure woman he'd just jarred. "Forgive me, young lady," he said to the woman, using his most charming, educated accent. She was far from young, but it was difficult to place an age, as her hair was tied back in a bun so tightly, it served to provide a temporary facelift. She stood a little below his shoulder line and stared intently with her gaze unwavering. Her immaculate black pencil skirt and jacket were the perfect accompaniment to her elegant white blouse. She was far from impressed by the insincere flattery and slowly moved her head with disdain. He was affronted; he wasn't used to women resisting his charisma, a point his companion was eager to point out to his great amusement. He shuffled uncomfortably; clearly the alpha male in the boardroom, but now uneasy and in an unfamiliar place. She had an aura about her, and as the man struggled to think of a further quip to satisfy his ego, he thought better of it. He bowed his head in submission, like a scolded schoolboy, as the air of bravado quickly deserted him. The train eased to her stop, and she leaned forward to retrieve her exclusive handbag, securely positioned between her designer shoes. She gave the man one final glance before leaving the train to a welcome burst of cooler air.

She left the station and took a short walk to a tedious row of terraced houses, which stretched into the distance. She was unimpressed, and took a moment to check the address stored on her phone. The houses were uniform in appearance, but they differed in their cosmetic upkeep; some were neat, while others had all manner of debris stockpiled in the compact, concrete yard at the front. One property stood out like a cat at Crufts, and even without checking the number on the door, she knew this would be her destination. It was an oasis of luscious green shrubs and a staggeringly beautiful array of flowers. It was difficult to accept that the courtyard was the same size as the neighbouring houses; the floral magnificence made the space appear considerably more generous — much like the inside versus the outside of a Tardis. It was hard to not be impressed, and as she pushed open the substantial iron gate, the scent of the blooms brought the indication of a smile to her face.

She rattled the polished brass knocker impatiently and became frustrated when a response was not immediate. She moved forward for a further barrage when the door creaked slowly open. An unshaven face appeared from behind the door and the daylight that hit his face caused him to strain his eyes. He stared for a moment and without a word, he slammed the door shut. An awkward silence ensued before the door slowly opened again, revealing a man who'd clearly just woken. His shoulder-length brown hair was unkempt, and flattened on one side with the imprint of his pillow. He wore a repellent green dressing gown which he fidgeted with to avoid exposing himself. He casually leaned on the door frame and looked up and down the street, as if looking for people stalking in the bushes.

"Una Jacob. What the fuck do you want?" he said, in a manner that was somewhat less than inviting.

She shook her head as she absorbed the sight before her. "You look a fucking mess. I mean, Jesus, have you looked in a mirror lately? You'd make Jeremy Clarkson look polished."

"Have you just come to insult me?" he asked.

"You think I'd come all this way to this shithole to insult you? If I wanted to insult you, I'd have picked the phone up."

"That'd make a change," he said, interrupting her. "You've not phoned me for months. So if you're not here to insult me, to what do I owe the pleasure?"

"Are we going to do this on the doorway?" she asked. He stepped aside and motioned her into the living room. Una was relieved that the cleanliness of the house did not mirror that of its occupier. It was basic and sparse, but neat and orderly.

"I'd make you a cup of tea," he said. "But I'm not going to."

Una sat in the single armchair, pulling out a notebook from her handbag as he sat on the sofa opposite. He sank into the cushion and his robe flapped open, to the disgust of Una, revealing the absence of any underwear.

"You used to be the housewives' favourite, and look at you now! You're unshaven, unclean, and overweight. Kelvin Reed, the darling of BBC Two, to this… *this*. You look like you should be sat outside a train station with a begging tin, eating a kipper."

"As you know, Una, the phone hasn't exactly been ringing off the hook lately!" he said sarcastically.

"And that's my fault?" asked Una.

"Yes, of course it's your bloody fault, you're my fucking agent!" he ranted.

She leaned closer, which caused him to instantly retreat. "After your deviant indiscretions, you're about as employable as a Jimmy Saville impersonator. Don't blame me, *you're* the one who got caught digging."

Kelvin looked confused. "It's *dogging,* not digging!"

"What?" asked Una. "I thought it was *digging,* and that's why there were so many innuendos, what with you being a gardener and all. What's the difference?"

"One is using a shovel to extract earth and the other is… oh, it doesn't bloody matter. If you haven't got any work for me, what are you doing here?"

"Well," she said, skimming through her notebook. "You owe me… twenty-seven thousand, five hundred and forty-two pounds."

He looked shocked as he processed the figure. "How the hell do I owe you that?" he protested. "You haven't gotten me work for months, so how do I owe you that?"

She handed him an invoice, which he carefully scrutinised before collapsing back in the sofa. "Aww, shit, Una. I haven't got a pot to piss in. I mean, look at where I'm living. That bitch of an ex-wife took everything, the house and the savings!"

"Don't forget your dignity," interrupted Una. "Mind you, I think that dignity disappeared when you were caught dig-dogging. Anyway, I know you're skint, as your statements still come to the office. Look, I'd happily never clap eyes on you again, but you owe me money, so I need you to *make* money. So you can understand my distress, then, when I hear you're turning work down?"

"What work?" he asked.

"The girls in the office tell me you were offered work in the Isle of Man?"

"That's not a bloody job. Five hundred pounds to gawp at a load of yokels breaking a world record? Christ, Una, I used to get paid ten thousand just for cutting a ribbon at a shopping centre. I'm not flying over there for five hundred pounds."

Una was clearly frustrated. "Look, I know you're not the sharpest pair of secateurs in the tool shed, but look at the bigger picture. You're not a complete and utter write-off. Hell, you used to be one of the biggest earners at the BBC. People loved you. We just need to get you completing some selfless task at a charity event where the press might just have a tip-off that you'll be appearing. Smile and wave your shovel… but, not that one," she said, gesturing to his crotch. "I think we've all read enough about that one."

"But how would the press know I'll be there, and why on earth would they turn out to see me?" he asked.

Una groaned. "Kelvin, *I'll* make sure the press are there, and trust me, this will be your first public appearance since your evening adventures hit the tabloids. And they're parasites, the lot of them, so you best believe they'll all want to get a good look at Kelvin Reed, right? So, then, you need to get something done with that mop on your head and smarten yourself up, and before long you'll be the darling of the middle classes once again and your calendars will be adorning the walls of horny housewives all over the country, yes? You can pay me back, and then I continue to take fifteen percent when the offers of work come flooding back in. I just need you to keep that firmly in your trousers, understood?"

Kelvin rubbed the untended stubble on his chin. "You know, for a repugnant, heartless bitch you're actually pretty smart. That's a great idea. I can see it now," he said, as he stood, filled with ambition. "Kelvin Reed will be back on the BBC, and back at the Chelsea Flower Show before you can say—"

"Close your bloody robe!" shouted Una. "The lion has fallen out of the cage, again. Oh, and just to make sure you don't mess things up, I'm coming with you!"

＊

Emma bounced around the coffee shop like a schoolgirl at Christmas. "He's coming," she said several times, clapping her hands with excitement.

"Is that what you say in the bedroom?" chuckled Jack. "Who is?"

"Kelvin Reed is. His agent just phoned to confirm the details and the date. She also said that she would be able to get the press in attendance so more people will know why we're doing it, Yay!"

Jack looked a little underwhelmed. "Are you not excited?" asked Emma.

"Yes, of course. I thought he was already coming, I mean, he's on the posters we had printed and I've been telling people for weeks that he was coming, so it's not that I'm not excited, it's just my excitement peaked weeks ago, when I first thought he was coming."

The shop was busy, not just in the lunch hours but for most of the morning and early afternoon. The Silver Sprinters and the social club were getting busier and as Emma had predicted, this resulted in more people coming in for food and drink. They were rushed off their feet, but they loved it. They worked well under pressure and the chemistry between them was evident. Such was the increase in footfall that they'd been forced to employ some help collecting and washing dishes over the lunch hour.

"I saw you chatting those old girls up in the window!" said Jack. "There's life in the old dog yet!"

Derek chuckled as he placed a pile of empty dishes on the countertop. "I think I'm too young for them," he teased. He looked smart in his grey flannel trousers and specially commissioned polo shirt, which Jack had made for him. Jack had a special enamel badge with 'Derek – Trainee' written on it. He was like a different man; he would still come in for his 8:20 a.m. cup of tea, but as soon as it got busy he'd spring into action. He was a man of advancing years, but his work ethic was exemplary; he could put a shift in that a man half his age would struggle with. He also knew how to speak to people and had a rare ability to make people of all ages warm to him.

Derek took the small ring binder from behind the counter and diligently wrote the details of the ladies in the window in it. "That's officially our forty-ninth and fiftieth members of The Lonely Heart Attack Club," he announced proudly. "And, I've signed them up for the Silver Sprinters."

"Shit, seriously?" asked Jack, looking through the binder. "He's right. That's amazing, I thought we'd be lucky to get half a dozen."

Emma smiled. "We may need to get a bigger place. We nearly didn't have enough seats for our speed dating event last night."

"Well, it wasn't really speed dating, was it? More like leisurely shuffling dating," said Jack.

Emma looked knowingly. "It certainly didn't slow Grandad down, did it? He was at more tables than a blackjack pro. He seemed to be getting fairly cosy with Hayley's grandmother."

"He did," nodded Jack. "I don't think the bingo girls were particularly happy, though."

"We might get our first wedding. Wouldn't that be wonderful," said Emma.

"She's a bit too elegant for him, and besides, at that age do you think they still, you know?" asked Jack. "Maybe I could ask Derek," he whispered.

"You bloody do, and I'll smash this plate on your head!" They both looked at Derek like proud parents as he worked the room attending to his customers. "It's pretty amazing what we've done here," said Emma. "We've not done anything earth-shattering, but it is making such a difference. Look at Ray, he's lost nearly a stone and looks like he is ten years younger. Derek has a job and an excuse to get out of the house, and we now have fifty older people signed up to our social club and you're a fitness coach for the Silver Sprinters."

"And I'm looking pretty fit, too!" said Jack approvingly. "I meant to say, that inspector chap — I forget his name — popped in earlier. Since our first social club and radio appearance, they've had thirteen calls from people who think they've been scammed previously or are currently in the process of being scammed. They knew it was common but even they were shocked by how many people were coming forward. They're going to set up a stall in the shopping centre, Tesco's, and a few other places and keep a couple of police in attendance to highlight scams. I've asked them to come along to the record attempt as well. They can keep an eye on that Kelvin Reed while he's here!"

Jack paused, clearly in deep thought. He was flustered and looked over his shoulder to make sure nobody was within earshot. He was trying to build up the courage to speak, and Emma was amused to see him squirming. "Emma," he said, struggling to look her in the eye. "When I was going to take you out for a steak, it was as friends. I know we've not really spoken about it, but after we nearly... you know."

"Know what?" asked Emma, enjoying the moment.

Jack blushed like a nervous schoolboy. "You know! Well, the thing is, if we were going for a meal, purely as friends, I'd be relaxed and, well, me. But now that things may have taken a slightly different path, I'm almost... almost, a little nervous?"

"Nervous!" laughed Emma. "It's me, you tool, why would you be nervous?"

He took a moment to gather his thoughts. "Whenever I meet a girl, I overthink things. My brain goes into overdrive and, sadly, that's when things go tits-up. With you as a friend I relax but with something more I start to think about what to say, act, wear, and do."

"So are you saying you just want to stay friends?" asked Emma.

"No," Jack assured her. "Not in the slightest. What I'm trying to say to you is, don't be surprised if I act a little… well, weird. When I go into dating mode, I'm hopeless, even more than usual. When I'm in dating mode I'm what you would consider a disappointment."

Emma looked at him sympathetically and leaned slowly forward, placing a tender kiss on his cheek. "Jack," she whispered. "Don't be such a bloody big tart. Honestly, just be you! There's no need to try and be something you're not. I know Jack Tate. I've known him most of my adult life, and, god knows why, but I like what I see. I really like the way you've embraced the work with older people. I like how you've become so compassionate and so wonderful, truly, a role model to society."

Jack groaned." Aww, what now?"

Emma tried to protest her innocence and feigned a look of shock whilst playfully pointing to herself.

"You," continued Jack. "I liked where you were going with that little speech. What are you buttering me up for?"

She didn't speak, but turned towards Derek, who was still diligently wiping the surfaces with impressive effort.

Jack rolled his eyes. "I've just got enough for a deposit on my new scooter."

Emma looked at him with puppy-dog eyes.

"It's silver, it's shiny, and it's got a horn that works. The bike starts first time, every time. It really is nice, and it's going to be mine. Ah, shit who am I kidding? I thought it myself, and was going to mention it to you."

Emma jumped up and down and continued to do the small girly clap thing she did. "You mean, we can…"

"Yes!" said Jack. "You can tell Derek that we want to buy his flights to go to the christening."

"Yay!" shrilled Emma, giving him a lingering warm embrace.

"What's happening to me, Emma?"

"You, Jack Tate, you're turning into a selfless person, who does nice things for other people."

"What's he done now?" asked Postman Pete. "And you've got a customer waiting while you two canoodle!"

Jack looked lightheaded, and it was apparent that the cuddle had more of an effect than just gratitude — a bulging point in his apron that Pete was very willing to point out. "You never do that when I give you a cuddle!" he said.

Jack wasn't fazed as he moved closer to the counter to seek cover. "Pete, it's been that long that I think even one of your cuddles would have set this thing off."

Pete looked confused, unsure whether to take it as a compliment, but he did attempt to arch his neck to gain another glimpse. He took an exceptionally small pile of envelopes and handed them to Jack. One advantage of the increase in trade was the decrease in needy mail, with people chasing you for outstanding payments.

"Why are you looking like that?" asked Jack

Pete motioned towards the post, and there was a white envelope with a resplendent crest for *The Guinness Book of World Records* proudly on the front.

"Ooh, Emma, come here," he said, waving the envelope.

He took a moment to read the contents. "It's our confirmation that the assessors will be here on Saturday, twenty-third August to validate our world record claim for the world's largest flower wall. We need to get to two-hundred-ten feet long with a height of no smaller than eight feet. Shit, that sounds a lot when you read it. A week on Saturday and we could be world record holders."

Dazed by the sheer magnitude of the task before him, he opened the other envelope. He glanced through its contents, and his overwhelmed-yet-hopeful demeanour was quickly replaced with one of disbelief.

Emma looked concerned. "What is it?"

Jack took a moment to digest the contents. "It's the bloody town hall. They've refused our permit to have the event in the Sunken Gardens."

"No. They can't, can they?" protested Emma.

Jack looked frustrated. "They have done! Ah, well. That's it, then, isn't it?"

"We can't give up now," said Emma. "We've put too much into it and we've raised thousands of pounds."

Jack looked slightly offended. "Don't be daft, I'm not giving up. We'll just find somewhere else to do it. Anyway, I'm more worried about where to take you on our date!"

Pete looked like his head was about to explode. "What? A date?" He did that girly clap that Emma insisted on doing, and he produced an equally feminine squeal. "Oh, it's so exciting! We could do a double date!"

"Who are you bringing?" asked Emma. "And are you sunburnt?" she said, referring to his bright red forehead.

Pete was slightly hurt. "You don't need to sound so surprised."

Jack had tuned out, returning to serve an elderly lady looking for a cup of Earl Grey tea. He didn't pay much attention to his own love life so the prospect of discussing Pete's was not overly appealing.

"I didn't mean it like that," said Emma. "I just didn't realise you were seeing anyone?"

Desperate to share his news, he quickly forgot the slight on his dating abilities. "Well... I'm not, technically. I've been seeing quite a bit of this man who is absolutely beautiful — tanned and very muscled."

"Ohh, who, and does he have a brother?" said Emma.

"You're spoken for! His name is Eric, and he runs the tanning salon next to the harbour. I drop his post in and he's totally been giving me the signals."

Jack heard the name Eric and tuned in. "Eric?" he said, as he passed over the Earl Grey. "Blond-haired and well-stacked?"

Pete's eyes widened. "Yes, but I haven't found out about the stacked department… yet."

"Sorry, Pete," continued Jack. "You need to buy yourself a new gaydar device. I know Eric from the gym, and trust me, he's not gay. I've seen his girlfriend, and she's absolutely smoking hot."

Emma looked a little hurt but, owing to the infancy of their relationship, thought it a little premature to chastise him at this stage. She would, however, store that comment for a later date.

Pete's shoulders dropped. "He can't be straight. I mean, he's immaculately dressed and looks after himself. Oh, I'm gutted. Emma, he's gorgeous as well. I've been in using his sunbeds every night this week. I've risked skin cancer for a bloody straight man."

Emma placed a friendly hand on his shoulder. "At least you technically got into his bed, if that's any consolation?"

"That's right," said Pete. "I don't need to tell people it was a sunbed! Anyway, I must continue, and I want to hear all about this date. In every detail!" he said, loud enough for everyone in the shop to hear.

"Well, that's one job we don't need to do," said Jack.

Emma looked blankly. "What job?"

"Telling the Isle of Man that we're dating. Because the sunburnt mouthpiece will tell the whole of Douglas by the end of the day."

"So, we're officially dating, are we? Can I tell all my girlfriends that my boyfriend is really dreamy?"

Jack smiled and threw his tea towel in her direction. He'd been racking his brains about where to take her on their first date, assuming she'd agree to the suggestion. He was still no further forward and now he had to figure out an alternate venue for the record attempt. It didn't need much, just space for a 210-foot wall and room for potentially hundreds of spectators and volunteers to hang up their flowers and potentially the worlds press desperate to get their first glimpse of the green-fingered deviant Kelvin Reed. *What could possibly go wrong?* he thought.

Nothing could disconcert him at the moment. He was probably the happiest he'd been at any stage in his life. The tables in their shop were full, and as he looked at Emma, he struggled to conceive that anyone so beautiful — both inside and out — would want to go on a date with him. He'd grown up, and knew what a fantastic opportunity this was for him. The next two weeks could shape his future and he was determined he wouldn't cock it up.

Chapter Ten

Emma had never had a car sent for her before. She climbed into the taxi with the destination unknown and it felt exhilarating. She'd no desire to be a call girl, but for a fleeting moment it felt like she was a high-class hooker being collected on behalf of a billionaire oil baron. The questionable personal hygiene of the driver soon brought her back to reality like she'd been hit with smelling salts. He was pleasant enough, but Emma was abnormally quiet. She was nervous; not only was it her first date in months, it was a date with Jack. She'd spent the afternoon desperately searching for a clue of their destination, if only to know how to dress, but Jack had given nothing away other than telling her to dress warmly. This had thrown her, as she'd had a skimpy but elegant dress singled out for their first date. But she had to err on the side of caution, instead opting for jeans and comfortable boots, and fortunately it was a relatively mild evening, as it turned out. As for Jack, he was hopeless at keeping secrets, so the fact she had no idea where she was going impressed her, and every time the car should happen to slow, she wondered if they'd reached their destination.

In addition to the TT races, the Isle of Man is also famous for its railways — both steam and electric — and Emma smiled as the taxi eventually pulled up to the electric tram terminal, a railway that had connected the Island's capital, Douglas, with Laxey in the east and Ramsey in the north of the Island. The tramcars were the epitome of Victorian workmanship, with some closed to the elements and others open for the adventurous to enjoy the bracing Manx breeze. She'd loved travelling on the trams as a child, but like many things on your doorstep, it'd been years since her last trip.

Jack emerged from a bus shelter as the taxi came to halt. Like a gentleman, he opened the door for her, and the smell of the driver caused him to recoil.

"That's not me," she whispered, discreetly pointing in the general direction of the driver.

Ordinarily, Jack would have made a quip about Emma not wearing enough deodorant, but he resisted. He paid the taxi driver and closed the door as soon as possible.

"You look lovely," said Jack.

"No, I don't," protested Emma. "I'm dressed warm, as instructed. So... where are we going?"

"All will be revealed, but I hope you're hungry," said Jack, ushering her to climb aboard the rear carriage, which fortunately for 'it's freezing in here' Emma, was a closed one.

Jack was dressed in a pair of smart dark denim jeans with a light blue hoody, and took a seat at the rear of the carriage. He looked towards the ticket inspector, and as soon as the fellow's back was turned, Jack produced two miniature bottles of champagne and two plastic flutes which he'd smuggled down his top.

As the signal was given to leave the station, the inspector gave a final peep on his whistle. Jack used the flurry of activity to pop the corks. "Cheers!" he said, filling the glasses.

He thought they had the carriage to themselves until the final moment when an excitable couple jumped aboard. They were fairly old and judging by the accents, were visitors to the Isle of Man. They took separate seats at the front of the carriage so they could each have a window seat, and by their attire and binoculars, they were clearly train aficionados. The tram burst into life and pulled up the slight gradient out of Douglas and towards the next stop in Laxey, where they would alight to join the mountain railway — another electric tram — that concluded at the Isle of Man's highest point: Snaefell Mountain. The tram gave a window into the stunning countryside on one side and magnificent sea views on the other. It wasn't difficult to understand how Victorian tourists would have been captivated by both the technical brilliance to build the railway and by the scenery, which it framed so well.

"I love this," said Emma, with a beaming smile. "Champagne and that view. I always feel nostalgic when I come on this. I'd love to have seen the Island in its heyday."

The motion of the tram was hypnotic and without notice, Emma removed one hand from her glass and placed it on top of Jack's as they continued to absorb the sea views.

"It doesn't feel weird?" said Jack.

Emma looked puzzled. "What doesn't?"

"This… us… It doesn't feel weird. I was worried that I'd feel like we were uncomfortable, but I don't, I feel at ease."

Emma smiled and increased the grip she had on his hand. "It feels nice!"

Jack paused, clearly building up to another question. "Emma," he said sheepishly. "Do you think it would be weird to see each other… naked?"

She nearly spat her champagne over the seat in front. "Naked! You're being a bit presumptuous, aren't you?"

"No… sorry, I didn't mean it that way. I wondered if you thought it would be weird to see me naked, or if it would feel like you were looking at your best mate, in the buff."

"Jack, I've seen you naked dozens of times. Are you forgetting the dressing room incident?"

"True," said Jack. "But what about seeing the 'old chap,' as it were? Do you think that would be strange?"

"Seeing it?" laughed Emma. "I felt it prodding into me when I gave you a cuddle in the shop."

Jack blushed. "Oh, I thought I'd got away with that. It's been a while, so it doesn't take a lot to kick it into action."

"Oh, thanks!" said Emma. "And if I'm being honest, I wasn't that impressed. In fact I nearly didn't come tonight!"

"I told you I was a disappointment!" laughed Jack. "But at least you now know what you're getting, I suppose."

"Again, somewhat presumptuous! Besides, you were looking at Pete at the time?"

Jack shrugged his shoulders. "Well, it's that postman uniform, it really does it for me."

The champagne bottles were soon emptied under the nose of the inspector. They felt like wayward schoolchildren at the back of the bus. "Do you think we'll end up like them?" asked Emma. "All old and cute, happy in each other's company?"

Jack was surprised, but the thought was a pleasant one for him. He smiled at Emma and then at the elderly couple now attached to their binoculars like wartime observers. "it wouldn't be the worst thing, would it? We'll be retired with a string of coffee shops and you'll still be disappointed by the size of my appendage."

"But, hopefully not your bank balance!" said Emma.

The tram soon pulled into the Laxey station, where they alighted to join their next tram. As they pulled out of the quaint mining village, with views of the famous Great Laxey Wheel, the lush glens and valleys were replaced with the vast hills and views towards the Island's only mountain, Snaefell. The scenery was sublime, to Ramsey in the North and back towards Douglas from where their journey had commenced. Emma was pleased she chose a warm layer, as the temperature dropped noticeably the higher they climbed. Their elderly travelling companions had joined them for the final leg of the journey and looked agape as they absorbed the rolling Manx countryside. The lights flashed to bring vehicles crossing the mountain road to a halt and as they crossed at the Bungalow section of the TT course, Emma waved to the passengers whose journey had come to a temporary halt. It was a highlight for children to see the tram passing by and the tradition of waving was one instilled in her as a child and one she was pleased to continue. She nudged Jack in the ribs to ensure his participation.

Standing on the highest point of the Island it felt like you were on top of the world. It was evident from this position how little the Island had been affected by development. There was not a house in sight, apart from the occasional disused stone farm building. It was a warm evening, but the wind was a little cooler at that altitude.

Jack took Emma by the hand and escorted her towards the café, which catered for the frequent influx of tourists throughout the summer months. Apart from half a dozen people they were alone on the mountain and for a moment she felt like Maria in *The Sound of Music*, but she resisted the urge to burst into song.

"Dinner awaits, my lady," said Jack, reaching for the door handle. He gave it a gentle push, and then a slightly firmer one, but it remained closed. Emma pressed her nose against the glass. "There are no lights on, and I can't see anyone in there. Jack, I hate to say this, but I think it's closed."

Jack took a step back and in desperation walked to the rear of the building to see if there was an alternate entrance.

"Aww, shit!" he said, sitting on the grass. "The bloody place is shut!"

Emma could sense the disappointment and joined him on the grass. "It's fine. I mean, look at that view! We can get something to eat when we get back."

"I know, but it's just I really wanted everything to go to plan. When I phoned, they said they didn't take reservations and just to turn up. Well, I've done that and they're sodding well closed!"

"Come on," he said. "We may as well take a walk to the highest point. Hopefully I don't get that wrong!"

A narrow path directed them to the highest point, and they couldn't help but admire the elderly couple who were now sat on a large tartan rug enjoying a flask of tea and a plate of sandwiches. "I should have taken some tips from them!" said Jack. "Think they'll throw a sandwich our way?"

Emma approached the crest of the hill, taking in a deliberate lungful of the fresh mountain air. "Isn't it…" she began, but then paused. "Hang on, what the hell is that?" she said. She took a cautious step forward, squinting her eyes. "Jack, come here. Look at that!"

With Jack's hand in hers, she stepped forward with increased confidence. She looked at Jack with a heavily confused expression. "Does that look like a table?"

"Don't be daft!" he said.

"It is!" she said, moving closer. In contrast to the green hills, there was a small table covered by an immaculate white cloth. A solitary candle flickered from a tall storm lamp positioned directly in the middle, and two chairs sat opposite each other.

"Please," said Jack, drawing one of the chairs back. "Your table is now ready!"

Emma was stunned. She accepted the offer and sat at the top of a mountain on her own private dining table. It was deathly quiet; not even the sound of the traffic below would venture to this altitude.

"What is all this?" asked Emma, with a huge smile.

"I told you I was taking you out to dinner, so I am." With that, he also took a seat and retrieved an ornate silver bell from beneath the table. With a gentle shake the noise echoed in the breeze and a moment later a man appeared from further down the hillside.

"Pete," she laughed. "Is that you?"

"*Pierre,* this evening, madame," he said, in an awful impersonation of a French accent. He was dressed in a white tuxedo with an overly flamboyant pink ruffle on the shirt and the most decadent leopard print shoes. "The menu this evening will be pear and endive salad for starters, a chicken, Roquefort, and walnut salad for mains, and then a lovely crumble aux pêches for dessert. Can I get you a glass of red wine?"

Emma couldn't stop laughing and was in a state of total shock. She looked for a bottle of wine but there was nothing. She playfully agreed and nodded her head. Pierre clapped his hands above his head and a further gentleman appeared from further down the hill. She stared in disbelief as the man had a silver serving dish with a bottle of wine and two glasses on it. As he moved closer Emma shook her head and placed both her hands on her cheeks. "Derek!" she called out. "What are you doing here?"

Derek didn't move as quickly as Pierre, but he eventually appeared with the expensive bottle of red wine. He cleared his throat and with an obviously rehearsed speech, he said in an equally awful French accent, "My name is Marcel, and I will be your wine waiter for this evening."

"You look wonderful, Der– I mean, Marcel!" said Emma, admiring the purple velvet jacket with matching velvet dickie bow.

Emma was incredulous. "I honestly cannot believe this, Jack. How the hell have you done this?"

Marcel and Pierre retreated before returning with two plates of food, perfectly prepared and impressively heated, despite any obvious means of cooking. Jack was quiet, just admiring the moment and the wonderfully warm smile on Emma's face.

"Madame!" said Pierre. "My apologies, I have forgotten the music." Once again, he raised his hands above his head and clapped his hands. A third man appeared, and it took a moment, but the sound of a beautiful violin filled the mountain air. Emma was speechless as she looked in bewilderment at Jack. She composed herself. "Bloody hell, Ray, is that you? I didn't know you could play the violin."

He halted his performance. "Ah, *bonjour*. My name is Antoine, madame," he said, in possibly the worst French accent of the three. He also wore a jacket, but his was dark-green velvet, with matching dickie bow, and it was obvious they'd been to the same charity shop. Despite this, Antoine continued to play a most wonderful rendition of Bach's "Ciaccona" to perfection.

"You've raised the bar here, Mr Tate. I'll expect you to top this at our next date."

"So there'll be a next one?" asked Jack.

"Well, maybe. I'll have to see what the pudding is like before I commit. Aww, how adorable does Derek look and how happy!"

"So you like this?"

"Jack, it's surreal. It's like I'm in some sort of crazy dream — crazy, but nice! This is one of those dates you read about in *Hello* magazine, and when you read it, you're thinking, *yeah, okay, lying to impress your friends*. But, here we are. How did you do it?"

"Trade secrets. I could tell you, but... you know the rest."

A remarkable byproduct of being more selfless in life was that people wanted to help you without prompting or without payment. One of the Silver Sprinters owned a restaurant in Douglas, and they were delighted to get involved. Pete was in his element, once again, and loved anything that screamed dramatic effect. He stood with Ray and Derek and watched as the romantic couple enjoyed their meal. It was a wonderful location and he covertly took photographs to capture the moment.

"What about you, Ray? Stunning!" said Emma.

"It was beautiful," said Derek, his voice breaking with emotion. "Truly wonderful. My late wife was very fond of the violin, and she'd have been absolutely captivated by that performance. You're very talented."

"Thank you," said Ray. "It's been years since I played. I'd forgotten how much I enjoyed it and how much people enjoyed hearing it."

Pete pulled out a beret from his inside pocket as it was time for the final course. All that was missing from his repertoire was the string of onions around his neck. He very nearly broke character as he topped up the wine glasses, but he recovered with precision.

The last tram of the evening had arrived, and the driver gave them the signal that he'd soon be leaving. The chef appeared from his temporary residence in the 'closed' café and was greeted by a standing ovation from Jack and Emma. Pete's ears pricked up like an agitated cat; applause was like a magnet, and he was quick to accept the appreciation. After a brief encore, he stepped aside and introduced his fellow cast members. Emma was caught unexpected as a tear fell down her cheek. "Thank you. Thank you all. What a wonderful evening and it's truly one I won't forget."

The driver gave a further burst on the whistle to indicate his imminent departure and the dinner party rushed to collect all of their belongings.

"Wait!" shouted Emma. "We need a photo before we go. Would you mind?" she said to the chef.

Emma and Jack took their seats again as Pete stood behind the table, flanked on either side by Ray and Derek with the violin positioned in the centre of the table.

"Cheese!" shouted the chef.

"*Fromage!*" boomed the collective response.

Hayley hung on every word. "My god, who'd have thought Jack could be so romantic?"

Emma nodded as she reached for the painkillers under the counter. "I know. Honestly, it was magical, and you should have seen the rest of the boys all dressed up in their little tuxedos, it was adorable. Unfortunately, my head feels like there's a boxing match going on inside. It was worth it, although I wish I hadn't agreed to open up!"

"So…?" asked Hayley.

"So…" laughed Emma. "Look, Hayley, are you okay with me talking to you about all of this? I really value your friendship, but also want to be sensitive to… you know."

Hayley rubbed Emma's arm. "Thank you! Honestly, it's totally fine. I'm really pleased that things seem to be working out for you — I promise. So… did he kiss you?"

Emma blushed and bowed her head. "Well, sort of…"

"How do you *sort of* kiss someone?" asked Hayley.

"Well, he dropped me off and like a gentleman escorted me up to the front door. He commented on how it had been a perfect evening and every other perfect evening he'd managed to muck up, somehow. He didn't want to jinx anything, so he took my hand, kissed it, and returned to the taxi. As they pulled away, he rolled the window down and shouted something about how he didn't cock anything up. So, not exactly a kiss, but romantic, I think?"

"Absolutely," answered Hayley. "That all sounds like the most perfect first date, astonishingly enough. Who'd have thought!" she said happily. "And have a guess at who *else* had a date this weekend!" she added, one eyebrow raised.

"You??" asked Emma excitedly.

"I wish, but, no," replied Hayley. "No, it was my gran and Jack's grandad!"

Emma was shocked and placed her cup of coffee back on the counter. "No way! Hmm, I don't think he said anything to Jack?"

"No, it came as a bit of a surprise to me. Apparently he asked her when you had that speed dating event on. I think she actually had three people ask her out on a date."

"She is so pretty, though, Hayley. I'm not surprised. I bet she was a real heartbreaker when she was younger. Where did they go?"

"Well, I think romance must run in the family. Apparently, he hired a horse and carriage and took them for a picnic in the country."

"Aww, that's so sweet!" said Emma. "I'm actually gobsmacked that they can both come up with such romantic first dates."

"I know! Look, I can see you're getting busy. I just wanted to see how the date went and tell you about gran. Oh, and the big flower order is due on Thursday, the wholesalers thought it was some sort of scam when I told them how much I wanted to order!"

"Do you think we'll have enough flowers?" asked Emma.

"I think so. Pretty much every florist on the Island is involved, but we should have enough sponsorship money left to go to the garden centres if we run short. I can't wait! Seeing a wall of flowers over two hundred feet long is going to be something special. And to get a world record… it's so exciting! I looked at the forecast for the weekend and it looks likely for brilliant sunshine."

"Fingers crossed!" said Emma. "When does Kelvin come over?"

"Friday night," said Hayley, walking towards the exit. "But I'm leaving him to it. I think he's bringing his agent with him, as well. Ah, Casanova!" said Hayley, crossing paths with Jack. "I've just been hearing all about your date!"

Jack smiled and closed the door for her. "Do you think she's jealous of me?" he asked of Emma once Hayley had exited.

"No, I think you're all good," Emma laughed. "How's the head?"

"Fine, but Grandad has just been on to tell me he took her gran out on a date. She's far too classy for him. Do you think I should tell her?"

"Oh, she already knows!" said Emma, shaking her head.

"Oh, shit. Was she okay? I mean if that was my gran and that old bugger came sniffing, I'm not sure I'd be overly chuffed."

"She seemed fine and she was well impressed with your romantic endeavours."

"Yeah, I am a bit of a catch. All those women who rejected me over the years must be really kicking themselves!"

"I'll lock the door when they all come knocking, now get your apron, you've got money to make so you can take me on an even bigger and more romantic date. Oh, Hayley said that the flowers are all on track as well."

"Great, we just need a venue now, the bloody town hall is still dragging their heels."

"I thought they'd issued a permit?" asked Emma.

"No. Bloody red tape. We'll just go with the original plan, it's too late to change now."

The lack of a permit had caused a few sleepless nights. He was calm on the outside but was genuinely starting to panic. It was impossible to make alternate arrangements now and the joiners were due to start building the frame for the flower wall the next day. He didn't want to worry Emma, but there was every chance that without the permit the whole event would come crashing down. Everything else was on track apart from this one bit of paper from the council.

"Jack," whispered Emma, as she juggled the controls on the coffee machine. "Thank you for a wonderful night. It was the best first date I've ever been on, and... hopefully the last first date I'll ever go on!"

It took Jack a moment to realise what she meant, but when he did all the concerns about the permit were quickly forgotten.

"Are you… are you dancing?" asked Emma, much to the amusement of their waiting customers.

"A little bit, yes!" he replied. He took Emma in his arms and waltzed her from the tight confines behind the counter, into the main shop. He leaned forward and placed his hands on her lower back and behind her neck as she fell slowly into a classic pose with one leg extended. As he pulled her back upright, he gave her a gentle but tender kiss, as several customers gave them a round of applause.

"You're crazy!" she said. "And unless you've got your phone in your pocket, I think you might have the same predicament as last time," she whispered.

"My phone is over there!" said Jack. "And, yes, you may need to walk in front to give me some cover. But, please, do take it as a compliment!"

"At least Pete isn't here this time," teased Emma. "Unless you were thinking about him?"

"Thanks for that thought! And here's one for you, then— Hayley's gran probably had the same effect on Grandad as you've just had on me!"

"Aww, too much information, Jack!" shouted Emma, as she put a hot teaspoon on his arm. "Too much!"

Chapter Eleven

Several lever arch files were placed chaotically on a battered-looking desk. Papers had spilt onto the floor and covered the tired, well-worn floor tiles. More files were stacked on top of a broken cabinet in the corner of the room. It was clear that this office was not purpose-built, but a requisition from an old filing room, rather. No one would deliberately choose this as their creative space, as it was miserable and without natural light.

A dirty grey phone, partially covered by a McDonald's wrapper, rang several times. A stubby hand pushed the detritus to one side and with great effort lifted the handset. "This is Terry," he croaked.

The man sat with his phone pressed to his ear, listening intently. He was overweight and gave the impression of being an unhealthy specimen, sweating without reason. His hair was thinning which gave the impression of being older than he looked; his dated suit perfectly matched his drab surroundings.

"What do I want with that deadbeat?" he asked. "Kelvin Reed? What good is he to me now? His career is already down the pan. If you expect me to give you two hundred pounds for that piece of shit, you can fuck right off!" he said, getting slightly more animated.

He threw the phone back onto its cradle and collapsed back into his seat. He placed his hands on the back of his head and the faint outline of a sweat stain was visible under his arms. Terry Trimble was a veteran of Fleet Street and one of the most despised journalists in the industry. He was without a moral compass and garnered a reputation as being a 'bottom feeder' — one who would do anything to get a story, regardless of how stretched the truth, or how questionable the source of the information was. It was a miracle he'd survived the recent press scandals, as those in the know, knew he was the centre of anything unsavoury. He'd been at the *Daily Times* for three years and in terms of quality news outlets, it was repugnant. The paper and in particular, Terry, had destroyed more careers than any other. No one was considered off-limits; Terry would've planted cocaine in Mother Theresa's car if it meant a front page. Unfortunately for Kelvin, it was Terry who broke the news of his alleged indiscretions and miraculously produced several 'eyewitnesses' to corroborate the claims. In addition, several grainy photographs were all that was required to destroy the career of one of the UK's most loved celebrities.

The door flew open, and a greasy-looking tall man stormed into the room. He looked around the room in disgust, and at Terry with even more contempt. "You were supposed to have something for page seven, three hours ago?"

"I'm on it, boss. I'm just following up a couple of lines of enquiry," he squirmed.

"Look, Trimble. I'm not taking the shit for your shortcomings. I've been carrying your sweating carcass for too long. Pull your finger out of your ass or you'll be lucky to get a job on hospital radio."

He took one final look around the room and scrunched his face in disgust. "And clean this shit pit up. It fucking stinks in here."

Terry wiped the excessive sweat from his brow and reached for the phone. His fat fingers mashed the keypad and he waited patiently.

"It's me," he said. "Tell me more about Kelvin Reed. Right, I know I wasn't interested, but now I am."

He paused. his head was getting more flushed.

"Three hundred quid? It was two hundred, five minutes ago."

He bit his lip.

"Fucking inflation? You're one unscrupulous shit!"

He backtracked.

"Okay, okay. Calm down. How long have we worked together? Three hundred it is. Now where is he going to be?"

He furiously took notes in shorthand.

"Where the fuck is that?"

He continued to take notes.

"Okay, this weekend? And what's he doing?"

He looked thoroughly underwhelmed.

"A charity record attempt? Who the hell wants to read about that?"

He listened intently and started laughing.

"*Ha-ha!* That's a great idea. Now I know why I've worked with you for so long. You're one evil bastard. *Disgraced BBC presenter in vicious assault on hard-working journalist.* I love it! I'll send the two hundred through now."

"Okay, okay, three hundred!"

He pushed the chair back and placed his feet on the table. His bobbled socks had a hole by each toe through which a yellow-tinged nail poked through. He reached into his desk drawer and like a cliché pulled a half bottle of whisky which was wrapped in a Co-Op carrier bag. He took a generous slug and wiped the excess from his mouth. His shoulders trembled as his laugh became increasingly more vocal. He was like a poor excuse for a supervillain, who'd just discovered the secret lair of his oldest nemesis.

"Sorry, Kelvin," he said aloud. "It looks like I'm going to destroy your career for a second time."

The captain gave a garbled apology about the short delay and assurances that they'd soon be underway. The plane was full, and it was hot, and people were getting impatient. It was early Friday evening, and there were a mix of holidaymakers and people returning from business trips. Una Jacob had lost the formal attire, but still looked commanding in dark jeans and smart blue jumper. Her brown briefcase sat between her ankles and her hands rested on a black notebook on her lap. There was a collective mumbling as the final passenger eventually appeared; even the air hostess gave him a look of disdain. He moved through the cabin and placed his bag into the overhead compartment. Kelvin Reed looked like he'd just stepped out of a Country Outfitters, dressed head-to-toe in tweed. He appeared too big for the seat and as he sat, he knocked into Una who hadn't broken her stare from the runway apron.

"You're late," said Una, in a calm but determined voice.

Kelvin was flustered as he struggled to fasten his seatbelt. "Yes, but not through my own fault. Everywhere I went, people kept stopping me. I'd forgotten what it was like, I've not been out for months!"

"You should be grateful for the attention," said Una.

"I used to be," he stressed. "But people come up to me full of smiles. They recognise me from the television, and then it dawns on them — or someone reminds them — about the stories in the press. Most people have forgotten what the bloody story was, they just know it wasn't positive. A woman in her eighties accused me of being a drug dealer last week. It's no wonder I don't go out anymore."

"It's when people stop recognising you that you need to worry, Kelvin."

"Look," he whispered. "Half the bloody plane is looking at me?"

"Don't be paranoid. They're probably looking at you because you were late."

Una didn't speak and wrote page after page of notes in her book. Kelvin tried on several occasions to instigate a conversation but every time he opened his mouth, nothing came out. He was good in his own company, but when he was with Una he felt uncomfortable as any silence wasn't natural. The offer of a drink from the trolley was a welcome distraction. "Whisky, please. Could you make it a large one?"

Una declined the offer of a drink with a dismissive wave of her left hand and continued writing. Kelvin quickly sank the whisky and tried to attract the attention of the hostess for another.

"It's a short flight, don't have another," said Una.

Kelvin felt like a child in her company; like he needed her permission to do anything. He'd survived for the last six months without her so wondered why he sat here taking instructions from her now.

Whether it was the whisky or years of pent-up frustration, but he moved his hand and placed it on top of her pen. "Do you not like me?" he asked.

Una was prevented from writing and looked pensively at his hand, slowly moving her gaze to his face. She maintained eye contact for what seemed like an eternity. She was tiny, but she was intimidating, and she took her other hand and pushed his away.

"Kelvin, to be honest, I don't have an opinion of you. And you should see that as a positive."

He looked confounded, but he was determined. "What does that mean?" he pressed.

"I tolerate you, Kelvin. That means I have no real opinion of you, positive or negative. I'm impartial and that's what makes me a good agent. Other agents would have dropped you like a hot potato, but I haven't, because I have no real feelings towards you."

"And I owe you a shitload of cash!" added Kelvin.

"Yes, there is that. Look, Kelvin, I'm in the business of making money. I have to spend my time with those that make me money. If they make money, I make money. Kelvin, I don't think you're down-and-out. Since I last saw you, you look like a new man. You've lost weight, cut your hair, and had a shave. Do I think your career is over?" Una reflected for a moment before continuing. "No, I don't," she said. "You owe me money. But if you were deadwood, I'd write that off, as successful agents don't like to be associated with toxic brands. It's not good for business."

Kelvin had a smile on his face as he replied, "That's the nicest backhanded compliment I've had in months!"

"Do you want to know what really grinds my gears?" said Una, composing her thoughts. "I have young kids sat in my reception for hours, desperate for representation. None of these record producers or theatre directors will speak to these kids if they aren't represented these days. They are hungry and will do anything it takes to make it big. I get pissed off when people like you have a successful career and go into self-destruct mode. I have another client. Clint Lee. You may have heard of him? His story was different to yours, but the end result was the same — people who have it all, and then seem to either throw it away or piss it all up against the wall."

She returned to her notebook, leaving Kelvin to reflect. He was unsure why, but he now felt positively upbeat. Una wasn't stupid. Far from it, in fact. And for her to have confidence in him, no matter how well it might be disguised, really gave him the boost he needed. He felt motivated, recharged, as he watched the Isle of Man coastline coming into focus before him, appreciating the view on offer as the plane banked over on its final approach.

The fasten seat belt pinged and the passengers began the scrum to dismount. A relatively overweight lady stared intently at Kelvin. He was used to attention from strangers but he felt a little uncomfortable as he reached for his hand luggage. She continued to stare as he joined the queue to exit the plane. As he approached, she clearly had a lightbulb moment, turning to her travelling companion. "It *is* him," she said, with a tone of mild disgust. "That gardener who got caught wanking on a bus."

There was a collective chuckle and once again, Kelvin began to wonder why he bothered to venture outside. "It wasn't wanking!" shouted Kelvin. "It was dogging! There is a bloody difference, you know!"

Una took a step back in an attempt to distance herself from Kelvin who was now puffing his cheeks in frustration. The hostess moved quickly to avert a situation and ushered the remaining passengers from the plane.

One man remained at the back of the plane, his head covered by a scruffy fisherman's hat. Terry Trimble watched the humiliating exchange with delight and chuckled as he replayed the conversation which he'd recorded on his phone.

"Excuse me, sir. Can you make your way to the exit?" asked the flustered hostess.

"Oh, yes, of course, sorry!" he said.

"I hope you enjoy your visit to the Isle of Man!" she followed up enthusiastically.

"Thank you, I will. I've got a feeling that this holiday is going to be the making of me," he said, with a cringe-worthy undertone that made the pretty hostess feel uncomfortable.

Hayley had offered to pick them up, as after all Kelvin was family, regardless of how distant. But Una had insisted they reject the request and instead arranged for a black Mercedes to pick them up. She was all about appearance, and Kelvin could appreciate where she was coming from. It would look better for him climbing into a limousine than a 'clapped-out Datsun Cherry' as Una had so eloquently put it. The driver — a cheery local called James — greeted them and escorted them to the car, parked outside. The repugnant woman who'd called him a wanker was stood waiting for a bus, so Kelvin had an element of pleasure, climbing into the back of a sumptuous Mercedes. As the car pulled away, Kelvin partially wound the window down and raised his middle finger in her direct eye line. James chuckled at the reaction of the woman who was desperately pointing out the indiscretion to her friends, but they were oblivious.

"She must be a fan, Mr Reed?" observed the driver.

"Yes, she was delighted to meet me. Hopefully she'll never forget the experience!"

"If you don't mind me saying, Mr Reed, it's a real pleasure to meet you. My wife and my mother-in-law are coming to see you tomorrow, they think you're fantastic."

Kelvin was delighted and gestured towards Una, who paid no attention. "Thanks, James, that's really good of you to say so. What do you think the reaction of the Isle of Man public will be towards me?" he asked, fishing.

James thought for a moment before answering. "People are looking forward to it," he said. "Not just to meet you, but the event tomorrow. I drove by earlier, and a big frame has been built and it looks like they're putting up bouncy castles and food stalls. They're really putting the effort in. I reckon there will be hundreds of people there tomorrow. And I've spoken to a few people about you, Mr Reed. You know, since it was announced you were coming over?"

James paused, causing Kelvin to lean forward, like a celebrity on *Top Gear* waiting to get their lap time. "And?" he asked.

"Well, most people think you're great. Not one person could tell me why you were in the papers anyway, and if you don't mind me saying, Mr Reed, the papers are full of shit anyway. My wife is a good judge of character, and if she likes you, then I think you're all right. She'll be down to see you tomorrow with the mother-in-law. Be careful, she and her mate are absolute bonkers, and they love you!"

Kelvin absorbed the stunning Manx countryside as they made their way towards Douglas. "It's quite a beautiful island you live on James, you're very lucky."

"Have you been before, Mr Reed?"

"Please, call me Kelvin. Yes, I was here about fifteen years or so ago. I was doing something for *Countryfile*, with John Craven. I thought it was a wonderful place then."

"You should move over," said James. "The Manx people are very friendly and I'm sure you'd be made welcome. As you can see, there is plenty of green space for you as well."

Kelvin smiled. "That's not a daft idea, James!"

It was only twenty minutes getting to Douglas, and as they drove on the promenade seafront, James pointed to a vast wooden structure, partially covered by a perimeter wall and with only the top visible. "That's where you are tomorrow, Kelvin. That's the Sunken Gardens," he said. "Your hotel is only up the road, so it's only a short walk." It was a hive of activity already, with tradesmen finalising the wooden wall and positioning a mesh fitting on which to affix the flowers.

Una had said nothing throughout most of the journey, and Kelvin was unsure if she'd perhaps fallen asleep. In truth, she was merely lost in thought. Kelvin didn't know it, but this was important to Una. She'd invested a lot of time in him, and as she said earlier, she didn't work with failures. If Kelvin was finished, it would be a slight on her character. One she'd certainly recover from, yes, but one which would be remembered by her detractors — of which there were many — just the same.

"Here we go," said James, pulling up outside the Empress Hotel. He jumped out of the car and attentively held the door for Una. He didn't receive a thank you, but he did receive the hint of a smile from her. Turning to Kelvin, he said, "We'll hopefully see you tomorrow, Kelvin, and if I'm with the mother-in-law, you've been warned!"

"I'll see you outside here, tomorrow, at eight a.m. I've arranged a press briefing with you and the organisers," said Una to Kelvin, walking a pace in front of him after they'd gotten out of the car.

Kelvin looked confused. "Don't you want to meet for breakfast?"

Una looked back over her shoulder. "I'll meet you outside at eight a.m.," she said, firmly.

Kelvin dropped his bag in his room, and as it was a pleasant evening, took a stroll along the promenade. He felt at home and for once relished being in a public place. Those that did notice him gave him a courteous smile or a polite request for a selfie. It was easy to get lost in the Isle of Man and be anonymous if so desired. Those with an ego would be easily disappointed that it didn't get tickled so often. He walked down from the main promenade to the vast sandy beach, removing his socks and shoes. It'd been years since he'd waded barefoot in the waves. A friendly Labrador was just as eager to join him in the sea, as it should happen, and playfully jumped around him in the water. The owner of the pet instantly recognised Kelvin, pulling a mobile from his pocket to eagerly snap a photo. "I thought you'd had enough dogging!" the man joked, laughing heartily, but then, quickly adding, and quite cheerfully, "Don't worry, I'm only kidding with you, Mr Reed! We're all looking forward to seeing you tomorrow!"

Even the insults over here were good-natured, thought Kelvin, and he did chuckle at how much that picture of him and the Labrador would have been worth to a lowbrow journalist. He re-joined the promenade and made his way to the Sunken Gardens. Being a gardener, his first reaction was to admire the beautifully crafted flowerbeds that spanned the perimeter of each of the gardens. It was a testament to the people of Douglas that such creativity had remained intact in a major town centre.

"Don't mind me!" he said, to the joiners working on the wall. From the taxi it looked vast; from here it looked colossal. He'd an idea of the scale required and looked up the videos and pictures of the previous attempt, but now he was here, this would take a herculean effort. The volume of flowers required to fill that frame was staggering.

"Kelvin!" shouted a voice from the promenade. For the last few months, whenever he'd heard his name shouted it was usually followed with an insult. He was pleasantly surprised to see a sociable face and be greeted by a warm handshake. "Kelvin, it's fantastic to see you. I'm Jack, one of the organisers of this and a neighbour of Hayley."

"Great to meet you," said Kelvin, enthusiastically. "You've certainly got your hands full here. It's quite a size!"

Jack looked overwhelmed. "I know, it's bloody huge. I didn't realise how big it was going to be. I just wanted to thank you for coming over, it really has helped raise the profile. I've been inundated with calls from the press over the last few days."

Kelvin rolled his eyes. "Sorry about that, Jack."

"No, it's positive, honestly, Kelvin. Most of them thought it was a great idea and as one of them said they've all got elderly relatives, so anything to raise the profile to protect them was a great thing. Two of the papers weren't going to cover it, but the journalists are coming anyway and bringing their families for a short break. Said they'd been here on holiday when they were kids and wanted to come back with theirs."

"Do you think you'll have enough flowers?" asked Kelvin. "You're going to need a fair few."

Jack scratched his chin. "We'll know tomorrow. Hayley has been great, and I think she's requisitioned every flower in the northwest of England. The sponsors have been generous, so we haven't had to scrimp. She seems confident. We've divided the day into four quarters, North, South, East and West, and are inviting people from each part of the Island to come along for a couple of hours each. They're welcome to spend the day, but this will give most people a chance to actually put flowers on the wall and really feel part of it. We've got schools coming along, and the kids have apparently been collecting flowers all week. A few of our Silver Sprinters — you'll get to meet them! — are running a bus service to bring the elderly down who want to come, but don't have transport. It's a real community event, and hopefully we can raise money for the vulnerable that fall victim to scams."

Kelvin looked a little reserved. "Sorry, Kelvin, I'm boring you, going on like this," said Jack.

"No, far from it!" Kelvin assured him. "You've actually humbled me. I'm so used to being kicked lately that I've forgotten that there are actually good, selfless people out there. I'm embarrassed to admit it, but when I was first asked to come over, I said no. Well, I don't think I was that polite about it, actually. But hearing you talk about this has actually restored my faith, somewhat. From my short time here, I'm starting to realise you Isle of Man people are a special breed."

Jack smiled. "I can't take the credit, Kelvin. I was a bit like you when it first came up. No, it was a friend, a very *special* friend, who first pitched it to me. She's wonderful, and you'll meet her tomorrow!"

"I'm looking forward to it," said Kelvin. "Jack, I want you to do me a favour, if you don't mind? The five hundred pounds you were paying me to come over? I want you to keep it and put it towards the fundraising, please."

"My goodness, that's a wonderful gesture," said Jack. "Really very kind of you!"

As Jack reached out to shake Kelvin's hand in gratitude, however, the moment was disturbed by a fellow, clearly intoxicated. "I wouldn't touch his hand!" the man shouted.

Kelvin smiled at first, assuming it was either a workman or a friend of Jack's.

"You'll catch something for sure if you touch him! He's a deviant!" continued the man, whose voice was becoming louder. He jumped onto a wall, and now looked down on them in the sunken garden.

"You don't know him, do you?" asked Jack of Kelvin.

"Not me, no, I don't think so. But it's hard to see from here," replied Kelvin. "Just some random arsehole, I expect."

Jack stood on his tiptoes. "Excuse me, mate, but why don't you fuck off!" he called up to rude fellow.

The drunken man continued to hurl obscenities and make lewd gestures, all directed towards Kelvin. "Woof, woof!" he shouted, at the top of the voice.

A few of the workmen building the frame now stood beside Jack. "Want me to go and punch that twat's lights out, you just let me know, yeah?" offered one skinhead joiner who looked rather menacing.

The man on the wall then stumbled slightly, and for a moment it looked like he may fall the ten-foot-or-so drop into the gardens. Kelvin tensed up, perfectly willing to help and to leap into action, regardless of the abuse he'd just received. But the man quickly managed to right himself, eliminating the need for any intervention on Kelvin's part, and Kelvin then largely relaxed again. "I was more worried about the flowers he'd land on, actually, to be quite honest," Kelvin explained to Jack out of the side of his mouth, to which Jack chuckled.

It slowly dawned on Kelvin, though, recognition setting in, and Kelvin shook his head. "Wait, I know exactly who that shitbag is," he announced. "That would be one Terry Trimble. Terry is what is known as the gutter press, and is also, not coincidentally, the idiot that published the stories about me in the first place."

Kelvin wasn't a fighter, but he was a big, broad man from working in the garden for so many years. Jack placed his hand across to restrain him, and he could feel Kelvin's heart smashing against his chest.

"He's not worth it," said Jack. "He's probably got a stooge somewhere, filming all this. What a scoop for him, getting hit by you. It's probably just what he wants."

The brute of a joiner, meanwhile, had skirted around and walked up behind Terry unnoticed. In an instant, he grabbed Terry by his belt and yanked him off the wall. "You better fuck off, mate, before I throw you into the sea!"

Terry may have been deplorable, but he wasn't stupid here. This guy was twice the size he was, so Terry made a hasty retreat, back to whatever rock he'd crawled out from under, shouting obscenities as he pissed off.

Kelvin looked embarrassed. "I'm sorry about that. Just when you think you can escape, idiots like that come out of the woodwork."

"He's adorable, isn't he?" remarked Jack wryly.

"Yes, a real charmer. Look, I'm sorry for the distraction, you guys clearly have a lot on. I'll see you in the morning?"

Kelvin felt somewhat deflated after the encounter with Terry. He nursed a nightcap in the hotel and a part of him was tempted to get a plane home and go again. He'd made an effort to resurrect his career, but at what cost? He'd been kicked and humiliated for months. Was it time for him to disappear back into the shadows?

Chapter Twelve

Emma had been awake since dawn. She'd scrutinised the forecast for days, but it was only when she opened the curtains to see glorious blue sky, that she could truly relax. So much preparation and time had been invested in today; it would have been heartbreaking if the weather had scuppered the plans.

She arrived early, surprised to find Jack already pacing the promenade like an expectant father outside the maternity ward. It would normally be desolate at this time on a Saturday morning, apart from the occasional dog walker or repentant reveller, taking the 'walk of shame' home. Jack read from a piece of A4 paper, mouthing the words, struggling to consign his speech to memory. From a distance, one would be forgiven for thinking he was somewhat of a lunatic, talking to himself.

"Morning, handsome!" she shouted, snapping him out of his trance. His eyes lit up and he marched over.

"This is it," he said, proudly. "I can't believe it's here and nothing has gone tits-up yet."

"Kiss of death, Jack! Here, I got you this!" she said, handing him a white carrier bag. He pulled out a bright pink t-shirt with a huge bunch of flowers on the front. She raised her eyebrows, waiting for a response. "Turn it over!" she insisted.

"The Bloomin' Wall record attempt," he said aloud, with a laboured enthusiasm.

She beamed. "I thought it sounded like—"

"Yes, the Berlin Wall… Love it!" said Jack, offering a high-five. "I see what you did there!"

"I've got one for all the Silver Sprinters who're helping out as well!" Emma was normally fairly excitable, but today she was like a kid on Christmas morning; she was bounding around like Tigger after he'd been eating sweets, and her enthusiasm was infectious.

The joiners had done a wonderful job on the wall, which was prepped and ready to receive its floral covering. On the main promenade, two men fired up their generators and two huge inflatable bouncy castles erupted skyward, to which Jack's eyes lit up immediately.

"If you're a good boy, you can have a go later," said Emma.

Jack chose to ignore the obvious double entendre, as he wasn't sure if he was at that stage in their relationship. "I met Kelvin last night. He popped by, after his flight got in," he said instead.

"Nice guy?" asked Emma.

"Yes, really decent bloke. It's funny. You read about someone in the paper, and you think you know them. You also think, because they're a celebrity, that they must be somehow impervious to criticism."

"Nice word!" said Emma.

Jack nodded proudly. "Thanks. Yeah, so, he was a nice guy. I actually felt a little sorry for him, and this dickhead gave him a bit of grief, which was out of order. He also said he didn't want the five hundred pounds and asked if we'd put it into the fundraising."

"That's wonderful. How nice is that!"

"I was thinking of putting it towards my new Vespa," said Jack, who, judging by Emma's expression, felt he must clarify he was joking.

Whilst the day was totally about raising money and awareness, Jack wasn't stupid. There would be potentially hundreds of people milling around — potential customers! He'd hired a van for the day which had a fully equipped barista station in the rear. He'd thought about buying one for years, but didn't know if there was any money in it. The person renting it to him knew he had a captive audience for the day, so was a little more aggressive on his pricing, but as Jack figured, it would be a great way to test the water. Emma was the quickest on the machines, and offered to man the stall, leaving Jack to coordinate everything else. Even though it was only 7:45 a.m., there were people forming a queue for their morning coffee, already.

Even though it was only a short distance from the hotel, Una insisted they take a taxi, and James, the cheery driver was happy to oblige. Kelvin looked impressive in his gardening gear, which was from a clothing range he'd had a degree of success with. Once again, Una made sense because the arrival of the chauffeur driven car pulling up gave the impression of success. Kelvin was a little bashful climbing out of the car, and gave a friendly wave to a couple of early-birds who'd come along for a closer look. Una placed a firm hand on his arm, shifting him from view, behind a parked van. Once again she looked impeccable, but had lost her casual attire for the more customary, stylish suit.

"There's no need to tell you how important today is for your career. Kelvin, I'm hard on you — I know that — but I want to let you know that I admire what you do. You're an artist."

Kelvin was sceptical. He felt like a child who was being given a lollipop, just as a needle was being thrust into their arm.

Una looked over her shoulder, as if checking there was no witness to her words of praise.

147

"When I walked up to your house, I didn't know what to expect. You can tell a man by the condition of his shoes — well, not yours, as they're covered in mud — but, in your case, the standard of the garden. I was genuinely lost for words. Stunning. I've never told you this but I've always enjoyed gardening, and before I was your agent I never missed your shows. It wasn't a coincidence that we met. I engineered it, because I knew you were something special. I wanted to work with you. I've already told you, if you were a loser, I wouldn't have anything to do with you. I'm here because you are the best at what you do and if you're sensible, we can get your career back on track. It all starts here. You'll do a small briefing to the local press, and as you know, I've had a couple of the mainstream press come over. There are a couple of film crews here as well. Take a breath before you speak, and you'll be fine."

Una took a step back and checked him over. "You look good."

Kelvin was a little taken aback about the unexpected kindness. It meant more, because he wasn't used to hearing it from her. He also knew she wouldn't bother with pleasantries if they weren't heartfelt. He felt uplifted.

Kelvin's appearance brought a sense of relief to Jack who hadn't slept much, worried that Kelvin may not turn up again as a result of the abuse he'd been subjected to the night before.

Jack motioned him over to the stage in front of the wooden wall.

"Morning, Jack. I love the shirt!" said Kelvin.

Jack smiled. "Don't worry, I've made sure you're going home with one as a souvenir of your visit!"

The temporary stage was two large cases of milk cartons requisitioned from Emma's supplies. She looked on with pride, as Jack took to the stage and raised his hand to attract the attention of those milling about, nursing their coffees. There were seven journalists, who were a mix of local and those from the UK media. Two TV cameras were focussed on him, but were not yet manned; they were saving their coverage for Kelvin. Jack looked towards Shelby, who stood with her impressive microphone pointed in his direction.

"Good luck!" she mouthed, raising her thumb in support.

Emma was bursting with pride; Jack looked like an important statesman, with the world's press hanging on his every word.

He puffed his chest out, and as he prepared to deliver his speech, three men in high-viz jackets moved towards the wooden wall. Jack assumed they were policemen, until one of the men identified himself as being from the council.

"Are you in charge?" the man asked Jack. "You haven't got a permit for this lot? We've told you twice, but you've just ignored us. You need to get rid of it!"

Jack was ashen, unable to string two words together as he climbed down from his temporary stage.

"Guys," he said, placing a friendly arm around the lead man. "I think there's been some sort of misunderstanding?"

"No… there hasn't. Have you got a permit to be here? Yes or no?" he stressed.

There were a few mumblings from the collective audience who were unsure what the issue was, and Jack's charm offensive was clearly faltering.

The men were beginning to lose patience. "You need to get rid of this, or we do," he insisted.

"C'mon, guys… I mean… fuck," he said, his voice now bordering on the pathetic.

Una marched towards the stage, all but knocking Jack from it. It was remarkable; as soon as she presented herself, people stopped talking. It was like the teacher walking in on a class of rowdy schoolchildren. Jack hadn't met her and could only assume she was with Kelvin; whatever she was about to say, she was his last hope.

"Welcome," she announced, in a confident and friendly tone. "Firstly, thank you for coming to the beautiful Isle of Man. Today is not only about having a fun day and hopefully getting us all into the record books. Today is also about raising a lot of money for a very worthwhile charity."

The council workers were baffled, wondering if she'd heard what they'd actually said.

Una spoke slowly and deliberately, like a seasoned politician. "We all have elderly and vulnerable family members and friends, some who have been or will face being scammed or victimised. With the help of you, the media, we can hopefully get the message out to a wider audience. We can make a difference."

The council workers moved forward once again, and Una pointed directly at them. "Today is about community spirit, and I'd like to offer our collective gratitude to these wonderful men from Douglas Council."

The men stopped and exchanged confused glances.

Una pointed at them and started clapping. "Civil servants come under a lot of criticism at times, but these wonderful, kind men have given up their Saturday to come and help this charity event. A charity event which will raise thousands of pounds for the vulnerable here in the local community — many of whom these men will personally know — and help countless numbers of people across our country. When the schools of the Island, and the elderly, on a rare day out, come to visit us and place flowers on this... this, Wall of Hope, it is down to the efforts of people like these fine gentlemen. I want you to take a moment to recognise them and thank them for helping make this charity event happen."

With that, the cameras turned to them, and a collective round of applause was offered in their direction.

The confused glances continued, but the man who appeared to be the foreman rolled his eyes and began to graciously accept the attention.

Una calmly moved to one side, allowing Jack to reclaim his throne. He was dazed and confused, and continued where she'd left off.

"Okay, yes, I'd like to echo those comments. Wonderful people," he said. "We've got a very special guest here to help us, and to cut the ribbon, as it were. He's one of the country's best-loved gardeners. Mr Kelvin Reed!"

Kelvin was nervous; after all, it was the press that had destroyed his career and here he was, once again at their mercy. He was ultimately a performer and the cameras and press didn't faze him, but rather the perception of those watching. After all, the press were merely a portal into people's homes and lives.

"Thanks, Una and Jack, for a lovely introduction. As Una mentioned, today is mainly about raising the profile of this wonderful world-record attempt and thereby showcasing the dangers and—"

"Pervert!" screamed a voice at the rear of the scrum.

Kelvin persisted admirably, but as the shouting continued the press began to lose him and look for the source.

Una marched towards the man and gripped him by the arm. "Trimble, isn't it?" she said, ushering him away from the rest of the press.

"I'd recognise those rodent-like features and small hands anywhere. I'd heard you might be coming over. You really are deplorable. Look, I'll keep this short and sweet. You either fuck off, or I'll phone my office and ask them to go into my safe. In that safe there are pictures of your father — Justice of the Peace, isn't he? — getting sucked off by a prostitute of questionable gender. You were off my radar last time. I'll make sure you aren't this time."

Terry went to speak, but the smell of stale tobacco and whisky caused Una to retreat. He started to laugh. "I don't care about that old twat. In fact, if you give me the pictures, I'll print them myself."

He moved towards Kelvin, and motioned for him to come closer. Kelvin was hesitant, but eventually climbed down. Never had Kelvin wanted to strike another human being as much as he did right then. Even the collective press were disgusted when they realised who it was. Terry was abhorrent, especially to those in the press who were trying to steer the industry through a challenging period; Terry was old school, and not what they wanted as representative of the industry.

"Kelvin," Terry whispered. "You know those witnesses who destroyed your career? Guess what… I paid them all. I've been tapping your phone for years. How did you think I knew where you were? And guess what else… I also know your little secret!"

Kelvin was a broken man. He looked down at his feet and began to shake with rage. Even the hardened members of the press were sympathetic. He took a step back and as if in slow motion, Terry Trimble closed his eyes in sweet anticipation of the impending punch.

Trimble felt a searing pain, but not from his face. His legs buckled forward, and he collapsed in front of Kelvin. Jack hovered over him and casually discarded the brush handle used to inflict the blow.

Terry cowered on the ground. "He just assaulted me, and it's all on camera!"

One of the press gave a look towards the cameramen. "We didn't have them turned on, Terry. Awfully sorry! I think the microphone was turned on, however, and we've got your little admission about phone tapping. I don't know how you didn't get picked up last time, but we'll be sure that the tape is heard by the correct ears."

Kelvin resisted the urge to kick the pitiful creature huddled next to him. He stood in thought for a moment. "This is ridiculous. It has to stop. Now."

He approached the members of the press. "Look, this piece of shit has destroyed my life. There's something I need to tell you, something that he evidently is aware of. That night when he ran the story about me 'dogging' is a load of rubbish. I didn't even know what that meant. I was just in the wrong place at the wrong time, but people believe what they read. I had no chance once the avalanche had started."

He resisted the urge to look at Una, unsure if she'd be throwing him daggers. There was a collective silence apart from Terry, who continued to whimper.

"I was never into dogging. The truth is… the truth is, I'm gay."

Kelvin didn't know what to expect. He thought there would be an audible intake of breath, perhaps. But, instead, there was only a collective murmuring of acceptance and acknowledgement.

"The reason I was in that place is because the man I was meeting was also in the public eye, and we wanted to keep it private. Hell, I didn't know it was a place where people went dogging. This piece of shit must have tapped my phone and knew where I'd be and the next thing you know, I'm all over the front of his paper. I was married with a family and wanted to spare them the pain. I was caught between a rock and a hard place. Today isn't about me, and I must apologise to Jack that I've inadvertently become the centre of attention. Today is about having fun, raising money for charity, and hopefully breaking a world record. If that's something I can help with, I'd be delighted to do so."

One of the members of the press began clapping, on his own at first, until he was joined by everyone else in attendance. Una walked towards Kelvin and placed her hand on his arm. "That took courage, Kelvin."

Jack was in need of caffeine, and retreated to the van. "It's like the fucking *Jeremy Kyle Show* around here!"

Emma hit him on the arm. "Don't be mean, that took courage!"

Kelvin began to relax and was the perfect host for the first arrivals. Hayley and her team of volunteers arrived with a staggering array of flowers of all shape and sizes. The smell when the van door opened was astonishing, almost overwhelming.

She took two small bunches of flowers and handed them to Jack and Emma. "Here!" she said. "You should have the honour of placing the first flowers."

They posed for a picture before proudly weaving the first couple of flowers onto the wire mesh attached to the wooden wall. The two solitary flowers brought home the scale of the task in front of them. The promenade became a hive of activity in next to no time. The bouncy castles and candy floss machines were doing a roaring trade and Emma had a constant queue; everyone was upbeat and enjoying the day. People were bringing their own wonderful displays of flowers and placing them proudly on the wall. There was a prize of £100 for the most impressive display, so the competition was friendly but fierce; there were reputations on the line as the majority of florists on the Island wanted to stake their claim as the finest. Those who didn't bring their own, could buy flowers for a small donation and make their own bouquets. People were writing notes to loved ones and attaching them, before putting them on the wall. They'd expected it to be busy, but Jack was overwhelmed with the success. He'd told the Silver Sprinters to come about 11 a.m., but he could have done with them from 9 a.m. It was difficult not to be touched by the effort that people had gone to, and how it brought people together. Entire classrooms of children were coming down on their day off, with the displays they'd spent all week working on.

Kelvin was wonderful with the children, taking time to help them place their work cautiously on the wall. He was on hand to speak with anyone that wanted to discuss any gardening related issues or needed advice; he was the consummate professional and the public adored him.

"I'm enjoying this, Jack," he said, enthusiastically. "I'd forgotten how nice people can be."

Jack smiled. "I should warn you about something," he said.

Kelvin looked concerned.

"Oh, don't worry, it's nothing bad. I told a friend of ours about your news this morning. I hope you don't mind."

"It's fine. The press are here, so the entire country will know by lunchtime!"

"Trust me," said Jack. "If *he* knows about it, the country will already know! Anyway, my friend Pete is a big admirer of yours, BIG, and he's, you know… gay. He's gone to the garden centre to buy an outfit. I thought that I should, well, pre-warn you!"

"Thanks for the warning! It does seem a little strange talking about this in the open, at last. I'll need to get used to it."

"And the uphill jokes!" said Jack.

"Pardon?" said Kelvin. "Uphill?"

"Yes, you know. Uphill gardener!" Jack laughed nervously.

"Uphill gardener? I don't get it?" Kelvin said, deadpan.

Jack was on the ropes. "Well, it's, when, you get a… You're winding me up?"

"A little bit, yes. Sorry, I couldn't resist. I will give you credit for the first uphill gardener joke, though."

"Thanks, and well done, you had me there!"

Like watching a boiling pot, progress appeared slow. It was only when you moved away for ten or fifteen minutes and returned that you could see the development. The Silver Sprinters had arrived on the first of their shuttle runs, bringing the elderly from the nursing homes down. Like the schoolchildren, they'd spent the week arranging displays to put on the wall. Some of them weren't exactly clear what they were doing there, but seemed happy, regardless. The difficulty with the older visitors was the pace they moved. Jack was encouraging their participation, but conscious of the people waiting. Two women who were barely mobile stood and seemed to be discussing the attributes of each flower individually.

"Hello ladies," he said, using his charm. "Isn't it just beautiful? It's a wonderful effort, and look at all the people waiting to put their flowers on. If you'd like to watch from over there, they can put some more on for you to admire."

The eldest and shortest of the two women had a cloud of coiffured white hair. She adjusted her glasses, which were as thick as milk bottles. "Is that you, Bobbie?"

Jack looked behind him. "Bobbie?" He glanced at her friend, who was equally as short-sighted and offered no inkling.

"Oh, Bobbie, isn't it beautiful? Really wonderful," she said, continuing to admire the flowers.

Jack knew he had to be tactful. "I'm not Bobbie," he said, gently.

She took a moment to think. "Where's my Bobbie? He'd love these flowers. He always helps me in the garden."

Jack's heart sank; this cemented why he'd got involved in helping the elderly. From his brief conversation, it was clear how fragile they could be.

"I'm sorry, my darling. Was Bobbie your husband?"

She looked mystified at Jack and started to get a little overwhelmed. It was apparent she was getting distressed, and Jack used his most compassionate approach. "I think Bobbie may have passed on. Can I get someone to help you?"

"Passed on? Oh, no… how awful," she said, getting increasingly distressed.

Jack froze, and put a reassuring arm on her shoulder, looking frantically for their carer. It was a fair assumption that these two had not been let out alone.

"Are you with these two?" he mouthed gently, to a man dressed in a nurse's uniform.

"Look, I'm really sorry, but she's a little upset. The flowers reminded her of her husband, and she's gotten herself a little worked up."

"Oh, dear," he said. "I didn't think she was married, but not to worry, I'll make sure she's okay. They do get confused every now and then."

The woman, now in floods of tears, sought comfort from her friend. "My Bobbie is gone!" she wailed.

Jack felt awful and thanked the nurse. "When she calms down, will you tell her I didn't mean to upset her?"

"Of course I will, and thank you for looking out for her," he said.

Jack looked down to the name badge on the carer's chest. "Thanks… Bobbie," he said, cringing.

He retreated to the sanctity of the coffee van. "What've you done?" asked Emma, who was juggling coffee cups like a circus clown.

"I'm fine," he said, clearly agitated. "Just a bit of a misunderstanding."

The vibrating phone in his pocket was a welcomed distraction as he moved to the sea-side of the promenade. He listened intently and nodded his head. As the conversation progressed, he raised his free hand and used his knuckles to punch his forehead. The force left four distinct white indentations.

"Ah, fuck!" he screamed, at the lapping waves.

The flower wall was resplendent in the midday sun and the bustle of people resembled bees attending their hive.

"They're not coming!" whispered Jack, through gritted teeth.

Emma was bewildered. "Who?"

"The bloody Guinness record people," he whispered, so as not to alert those in his vicinity. "They're fog-bound at Gatwick and don't think they will make it today."

In a further tribute to Basil Fawlty, Jack began to hyperventilate and grin uncontrollably, projecting a shrill tone barely audible to a dog.

Sensing he was on the verge of a meltdown, Emma handed him a bottle of water. "Jack... chill... the... fuck... out!" she said, with her hands on his shoulders. "When can they come?"

"Tomorrow, at ten a.m."

"Okay, that's fine. Just carry on with everything. We'll know today that we've broken the record because the wall will be full. Tomorrow will just be a formality. It will be just fine. Now, take a deep breath and enjoy the rest of the day. I think you need to go and rescue Kelvin!"

Pete gave the appearance of a seasoned professional. He was dressed head-to-foot in green, sporting a pair of wellington boots with a dark pink trim that had no intention of gracing an allotment. He held his arms aloft, giving the gesture of a fisherman indicating — or exaggerating — the size of his biggest catch. Kelvin, ever the professional, listened intently and also raised his hands, but extended the size of his catch.

"They're fine!" said Jack, whose stress levels were beginning to plateau. "They seem happy comparing the size of their cucumbers. Did you tell Derek about the ticket?"

"No, I've not seen him today," said Emma. "And I'm a bit tied up here, so you should!"

A number of the Silver Sprinters had converged in the sunken garden. With the influx from the old folk's home, it was like a huge congregation of grey hair and slippers. As Jack had hoped, the day was evolving into a social event, enjoyed by all of the generations. Even the council workers, who'd nearly brought the day to a premature conclusion, were now embracing the day enjoying the inflatable castle.

Derek was deep in conversation with Ray and the others and appeared to be having a fantastic day. Jack tried to attract his attention through the crowd, but Derek was lucky if he could see five feet in front of him, and there was no point in shouting as his ears were as equally inept. He waved frantically until he caught Derek's attention.

"Jack," he said warmly. "What a wonderful event. I've seen people here today that I've not seen for years."

"That's great!" said Jack, pulling him away from the other Silver Sprinters. "So, Derek, you know how you've become good friends with Emma and myself, and also part of the team at the shop?"

"You're not letting me go, are you, Jack?" he said, with an anxious expression.

"What… no, no, of course I'm not. You're part of the team. Please don't think that Emma and I are sticking our nose into your business. But, well, we are. Thing is, we know that by being too nice, you've given most of your cash away."

Derek was confused and struggling to keep pace with the topic of conversation.

"Aww, Derek. I'm not overly good at the 'softly-softly' — this is why I asked Emma to speak to you. I'll keep it brief. You lost all of your money, so we've bought you a ticket to go to Italy for the christening… there!"

Derek looked more fragile than usual, like a sapling swaying in the wind. "Are you okay?" asked Jack, supporting him at the elbow.

Derek wanted to speak, but his voice broke every time he tried. His bottom lip trembled as he reached into his pocket for an immaculate white handkerchief. "Thank you," he said, his voice wavering.

Jack continued to hold his arm. "Ah, you silly old sod. You've got me all upset, as well," he said, wiping a tear away in a less refined way, with his sleeve.

That moment summed up what Jack had morphed into — a giver, rather than a taker. He looked with affection at Derek, a frail but wonderful man in his twilight years, and he took great delight in reducing him to tears. The money he'd used towards the ticket was his deposit on a new Vespa; never had Jack been so pleased to be commuting on his dilapidated, trusty workhorse.

The emotional exchange had not gone unnoticed by Emma, and when Jack caught her eye, she held both clenched fists to her chest and chewed her bottom lip; she blew him a kiss and hoped it would navigate through the throng of assembled people between them. Jack playfully shuffled with his hands, cupped like a wicket-keeper, ready to receive the gesture of affection.

The remaining members of the Lonely Heart Attack Club appeared and paid homage to the wall, under the careful scrutiny of Kelvin, who'd failed to distance himself from his new admirer. The dispatches with the day's news had evidently not reached the Bingo Girls — who were insatiable — and Kelvin was clearly their target for the day. "Oh, you're a strapping young man," said one, as Kelvin helped her fix her flower to the wall. There was no requirement for assistance, but she played the inept card with precision and as he moved closer, he felt a firm hand squeezing his arse. "Firm like a turnip," she said smugly to her friend. By coincidence, it transpired that she was the mother-in-law that the taxi driver had warned him about earlier. Pete gave the girls a barbed glance, slightly incensed that he'd not thought of that tactic.

By mid-afternoon, the crowds had begun to thin out. Their elderly visitors had been returned to their homes after a fun day out. Some children remained to take advantage of the bouncy castles and candy floss, and it was pleasing that the day had passed without incident. The Bloomin' Wall was the star of the show. The scale was dazzling and an assault on the senses. It was as if there'd been an explosion in a paint factory, such was the array of vibrant shades, and the magnificent scent carried on the breeze. Hayley had worked like a trooper and skilfully managed the conveyor belt of people desperate to play a small part in the proceedings.

"There is probably only room for another three bunches," said Hayley, beckoning Emma and Jack. "You should put the last few on!"

Jack shook his head and ushered all the friends and helpers into a tightly formed circle. "C'mon," he said. "We'll all do this together." Everyone leaned in, and between them, placed the final flowers onto the wall. Jack deliberately held one vibrant bunch of yellow roses to one side. There was one small space in the wall remaining. "This is it, guys. This is the final piece of what has been one hell of a jigsaw." He waved over one of the press and asked him to take a picture of the group as they all reached for the bunch of flowers that Jack held aloft, like Excalibur. "The Lonely Heart Attack Club!" shouted Jack, at the top of his voice.

"The Lonely Heart Attack Club!" they all shouted in a fit of giggles.

Chapter Thirteen

"Come on," said Emma, pulling Jack's arm. "And take your shoes off!"

"Emma... behave, my grandad is stood there!"

"It's a jump you're getting, but not that kind!" she teased.

Emma had bribed the bouncy castle operators with a coffee for a private audience. "Yes!" said Jack, kicking off his shoes. Emma loved the boyish innocence as he bounced like a coiled spring with limitless energy.

"Well done, today," said Emma.

Jack held his hand to his ear, causing Emma to move closer.

"I said, well..."

Jack pulled Emma towards him — kissing her — as they bobbed like corks in water from the motion of the castle, swaying. "You didn't do too badly, either. What a fantastic day!"

He gave her another kiss as the movement of the castle forced them even closer.

"Jack, have you got a...?"

"What? No, not this time, I've got my phone in my pocket."

"Are we going to get something nice to eat and open a bottle of something?" asked Emma.

Jack pulled a face. "I can't tell you how appealing that sounds, but I think I need to stay here."

"Eh? Why?" asked Emma.

"It doesn't look like the record people are going to get over tonight. I can't risk leaving those flowers unattended overnight otherwise there will be nothing left in the morning."

Emma was disappointed but understood. "I'll stay with you?" she said.

"No, you won't. You've been on your feet all day. Go home and have a nice bath and we'll do something tomorrow night. I've got a feeling a couple of the guys are going to take it in shifts and I've already heard Derek talking about popping home for his nice bottle of port. Honestly, we'll be fine, it's not cold. Is that okay?"

"Of course it is," said Emma. "You can share your war stories with the guys!"

Jack sat on a requisitioned deck chair and watched the sun disappear to the west of the Island. He'd been left with blankets and food and, more importantly, a few tins of beer.

He reflected on the day and briefly felt a little flat. They'd been full-on for weeks, and the excitement for all involved was palpable. It was genuinely a team effort and part of him feared that the comradery would be lost. He'd met a truly eclectic group of people, one he'd grown deeply fond of. He consoled himself with the thought of how many people had been touched in a positive way — including Kelvin's arse, which was likely to be still tender from the Bingo Girls; if Pete had his way it would be even tenderer.

Rather than being despondent, he thought to the future. There would be another challenge, another record to break. The club was growing in numbers. Maybe they'd need to expand, open more shops; global domination by taking on the corporate shysters. This was just the start for Jack, the shop, and the club. Rather than being a conclusion, he was determined that it would instead be a catalyst.

"I hope you like a drop of port?" asked Derek, taking Jack out of his trance.

"Derek, I'm glad you came back. Pull up a deckchair! I'm not sure about port, but it's a day of firsts, so I'll give it a go! Thank you for all of your help today, Derek."

Derek nodded and absorbed the sight of the flower wall with what remained of the failing sunlight.

"You, Emma, and Hayley, you're all kind people. Whatever happens in your life, you should know you've enriched the lives of a lot of people," he said, in a thoughtful manner.

Jack was humbled, and in that moment, he knew he'd be talking about the characters — such as Derek — to his grandchildren in years to come. It was funny how people on a completely different trajectory in life can sometimes be pulled together, and in doing so enhance other people's lives.

Half a bottle of port later and Derek had dozed off in the deckchair — even though he was only staying for an hour — and *how* was a mystery to Jack, as those chairs were uncomfortable as hell. The promenade was full of Saturday night revellers, but all in good nature with the majority stopping to admire the wall, and most throwing a few coins in the collection bucket.

During a brief lull in traffic, Jack took the opportunity to use the facilities in the pub opposite. Derek was flat out, so he took the remaining charity bucket with him for safekeeping and whilst the port was palatable, the thought of a cold pint was more alluring.

A huge moon cast a haunting reflection on the still water and created a perfect silhouette of the Tower of Refuge, in Douglas Bay. The air was still, but the smell of the flowers still hung in the air. Derek fidgeted in the flimsy deck chair as the wooden frame dug into his back; he couldn't get comfortable, and his shallow sleep was interrupted by the smash of glass. He opened his eyes and saw four boys and two girls stood in front of him, about six feet from the wall. They were drinking from bottles and listening to music from a mobile phone. He was still half asleep, but he quickly pushed himself into a standing position.

"What are you doing?" he said, raising his voice, pointing towards a pile of glass.

"Nothing!" was the collective response from the youths, who walked closer to Derek. In the blink of an eye, glass bottles smashed against the floor like a volley of gunshot. Derek moved back a pace or two, but the teenagers closed the gap. The calm of the evening was destroyed in a moment, as a noise like thunder echoed through the sunken garden. In desperation, Derek protected his head with his hands and tried to turn his back on the shower of glass. The noise was deafening, and such was the speed and veracity of the carnage, it was difficult for him to know which way to retreat.

"What the fuck are you doing?" shouted Jack, throwing his pint of lager to one side. He grabbed the youth closest to him and pushed him to the floor. He tried to protest, but the chaos ensued. Jack soon succumbed and had no option but to collapse onto one knee and also protect his head. He reached out to Derek, who by now had fallen on the grass patch beneath the wall. As soon as the noise ended, Jack leapt to his feet and again moved towards the youths. Jack was bewildered; they were in the same situation as he was, also struggling to take cover.

"We didn't do anything!" shouted one of the girls. "I was showing my friends the wall that I put a flower on today. We didn't want to wake him up so we crept in."

"What was the noise?" asked Jack, who was now completely confused.

"It's that idiot," said one of the group. "He threw a bin at the wall."

Jack took a step back to compose and assess the situation. What he thought were glasses hitting him like a revolving door, were in fact seagulls making a play for the contents of the bin. Chips and all manner of discarded food formed a carpet around the wall. A constant salvo of birds dive-bombed like the German Luftwaffe, taking advantage of an easy meal.

Jack helped the youth he'd gripped and apologised immediately. The youths were only there to admire their handiwork during the day, and show their friends what they'd been involved in. Jack felt awful, but they understood the confusion and that he was only jumping to the defence of his Derek.

"Shit!" said Jack, moving towards the wall. The metal bin had struck it with precision and pulled great swathes away from the supporting frame. It lay on the reverse side, leaving what looked like a tunnel of flowers and twisted metal mesh in its wake. The heads of the flowers had exploded, leaving a layer of petals on the ground that mixed in with the unwanted food. Roughly a third of the wall was destroyed or hanging on by a thread, with the birds continuing to cause additional damage.

Jack's anger turned towards the person who threw the bin. He ran up the stairs and looked further up the promenade. A man — clearly the worse for wear — progressed slowly and erratically, and it only took Jack a moment to catch up with him.

"Oi!" he shouted, but with no reaction from the man. Jack cautiously grabbed him by the shoulder, and, as he did so, the man swung 'round with a misguided punch. Any coordination he had was well and truly drowned by alcohol, and he collapsed in a heap. Jack turned him over to check that there were no injuries, but he was just clearly very drunk.

Jack stared down at him, struggling to place the face. "Terry Trimble! You piece of shit!" He gripped him by the collar and held a shaking fist close to his face. "You're not worth it," said Jack. Rather than throw him back to the floor,

Jack helped him to his feet and checked him over once again for injury, before he carried on his wayward journey.

The youths remained and used the lid of the bin to collect the broken glass. There were feathers everywhere, and with the ketchup from the chips it looked like a bird had fallen in a food blender.

"It was that bloody journalist, Derek," said Jack, slightly out of breath. "Are you okay?"

Derek stood with one arm extended against the perimeter wall of the sunken garden, and his back towards Jack.

"Derek, can I get you a seat?"

He didn't speak, and with a gasp of air, Derek dropped to his knees.

"Call an ambulance!" screamed Jack to the youths. "Now!"

Emma reached sleepily for her phone. As soon as she heard Jack's voice, she could hear the panic. "Is everything okay?" she asked, before pausing for a moment. "Okay, I'll meet you there."

The hospital was only a short drive, but it felt like every traffic light was conspiring against her. She drove straight past the car park and abandoned the car at the entrance. She was still in her pyjamas and her hair was a mess from not drying it completely after her bath. Jack stood at the end of a long, abandoned corridor and walked towards her.

She took him in her arms. "How is he?"

"I don't know," said Jack, desperately. "They took him away as soon as we arrived. He was clutching his chest."

Emma tried to remain strong, but the tears fell freely down her cheeks. "Oh, Derek!" she said.

A nurse furnished them with a cup of tea and Jack held Emma tenderly for what seemed like hours. It was late, and the hospital was quiet; they could hear every door open and close. They didn't speak much, but they were there for each other.

An older male doctor with a warm expression and kind face took them into a room. Emma was listening, but not absorbing the words. He escorted them into a room where Derek was wired up to a multitude of machines.

Jack sat on one side of the bed and Emma the other; they each gently took one of his hands. Emma leaned forward and placed a gentle kiss on the side of his cheek and squeezed his hand a little tighter.

Derek died in the early hours, surrounded by those who cared about him, surrounded by his friends. The nurse was wonderful with them and gave Jack and Emma all the time they needed. She gave them a bag with some of his possessions, but one item she kept separate. "I wanted to give you this personally. I didn't want it to get damaged."

Emma's tears were now flowing uncontrollably, and she sobbed so much her chest hurt. Derek had kept the picture from the top of Snaefell — dressed in his tuxedo — in his wallet. She gazed at the photo with great fondness and took great comfort from the huge smile he had on his face.

They didn't sleep much that night. Jack took it upon himself to phone Derek's family; he felt it would be more personal than someone from the hospital that didn't know him. They were devastated, but insisted on hearing all about the record attempt that Derek had been talking to them about for weeks.

Jack must have drifted off for a moment when his phone buzzing in his pocket woke him. It was the people from the Guinness World Records, who'd arrived on the Island and were on their way into Douglas. Part of him was tempted to tell them to stay at the airport as, after all, their record hope was destroyed. But they'd come all this way, the Guinness people, so he wanted to afford them proper courtesy. Emma and Jack made the solemn journey to the promenade, dreading the sight of the wall in the cold light of day.

"We'll do it next year," said Emma, as she placed a reassuring arm around his waist.

By the time they arrived, Kelvin, Hayley, and the rest of the Silver Sprinters were stood near the wall. There were tears and people consoled themselves, sharing memories of happier times.

Hayley walked towards them, and they shared a tender embrace. "I'm really sorry," she said. "Kelvin insisted on coming down to help us fix the wall, but, we couldn't. There is just too much damage to do anything with it."

Jack and Emma stood in front of the wall and the considerable hole that'd been cleaned up as much as possible. He apologised to the Guinness people for their wasted journey, but as he'd hoped, they were fine and offered to come over the following year if they wanted to do it again.

They all lined up in front of the wall, using it as a focal point for their collective grief.

Kelvin moved in from the rear of the garden, where he'd been diligently working on trying to resurrect the wall, but it was an impossible task. Instead, he'd used the discarded flowers to form one huge bouquet. He walked behind the wall and lifted it into place, positioning it in the centre of the existing hole, where he fixed it in place.

The tears from the group, which had not abated, fell in floods once again. Kelvin had taken the flowers, which were virtually destroyed, and created a stunning wreath with the words, *Derek – Our Friend.*

The funeral was a touching but lively affair, culminating in a party above the coffee shop. Jack was touched when Derek's family went out of their way to speak to them about

Derek's career and his early life, of which he never really spoke about. He was a character and now hopefully reunited with his beloved wife.

Jack was determined to make the day special and once again had used his meagre savings — destined for the bike dealership — to instead fix the missing letter on the sign, outside the shop. Derek had only worked there for a short time, but he'd have wanted the shop looking its best.

There were more than eighty people at the wake, a testament to the affection and friendship he'd formed over the years; he'd touched a lot of people. Jack cleared his throat and tapped the side of his wine glass to bring the room to attention.

"I just wanted to take a moment to raise our glasses to remember a special, wonderful man. We only knew him for a short time, and if I had the opportunity I'd have made it my mission to know him longer. He was a wonderful and kind man and I'd love it if you'd all raise your glasses in a toast."

"Derek!"

"Before I go, I'd like to say one more thing," said Jack. Emma was getting a little nervous as he'd had a glass or two of wine, and despite his best intentions, she worried in case he'd say something inappropriate.

"Derek was one of the founding members of The Lonely Heart Attack Club. There is an irony that he died of a heart attack." There was a collective groan.

"The thing I'm most pleased about is that he wasn't lonely. He was surrounded by wonderful people. We'll continue with the club and make it bigger and better and most importantly, we'll look out for each other. We'll make sure our friends aren't lonely!"

Emma walked towards him, and then nearly squeezed the life out of him. "That was wonderful!" she said. "You really are a big old softy. Derek would have been proud of you!"

୬

"Terry Trimble – Jailed for 3 Years" was the headline that got the biggest cheer in Fleet Street for a generation. The loathsome man had truly had his comeuppance when the phone tapping scandal finally caught up with him. There was a relief in the media and the hope that he was the last of the old guard and they'd be in a position to move forward. On the same front page — but a separate report — ran the story about Kelvin Reed securing a new contract with the BBC; perhaps the editor's ironic swipe to include both stories collectively.

Jack had the front page of the paper framed and it sat resplendent behind the till. He'd also had a small brass plaque made which sat above a chair in the corner of the shop: *Derek – a gentleman, sat here at 8:20 most mornings.* He was gone, but certainly far from forgotten and Emma fondly recalled her time with him when she polished the plaque each morning at 8:20 a.m.

Jack poured a glass of wine and joined Emma on the sofa. "Are you glad you stayed in this flat, then?" she asked, nestling into him.

He looked around the modest flat which now had an impressive overhaul, driven mainly by the small but effective feminine touches. "I am now you're living here," he said. "But you need to stop peeing on the toilet seat, and would it kill you to take the hair out of the plughole! Are you glad you didn't go to Singapore?"

She pinched his side. "You love me being here. I'm going nowhere. Now, shush, Kelvin is on."

Kelvin Reed had finally returned to mainstream television, a little over eighteen months since he fell victim to shambolic, insincere reporting. He'd been the king of Sunday night television for a decade and now he'd returned to this throne.

To their complete shock and delight, Kelvin spent the first two minutes of his new show talking about the previous eighteen months and how he'd nearly given up. He spoke about one of the catalysts being "the selfless and admirable efforts put in by unpaid volunteers to make the community a safer place, and one where the vulnerable felt less alone." He summed up the intro thusly: "To my good friends in the Isle of Man, and to Derek, who, sadly, recently left us... to my friends there, I'll hopefully see you next year!"

"We're famous!" shrieked Emma, with delight.

Jack picked up his glass of wine and gave a toast to the TV. "We'll get that bloody world record. Here's to next year!"

THE END

If you've enjoyed this book, the author would be very grateful if you would be so kind as to leave feedback on Amazon. You can subscribe for author updates and news on new releases at:
www.authorjcwilliams.com

J C Williams
Author

authorjcwilliams@gmail.com
🐦 @jcwilliamsbooks
📘 @jcwilliamsauthor

And if you've enjoyed this book, be sure to check out the second in the series: *The Lonely Heart Attack Club: Wrinkly Olympics*, and very soon, the third, *The Lonely Heart Attack Club: Project VIP.*

And if you've enjoyed this book, make sure to check out my other books as well!

The *Frank 'n' Stan's Bucket List* series:

The Seaside Detective Agency and *The Flip of a Coin*:

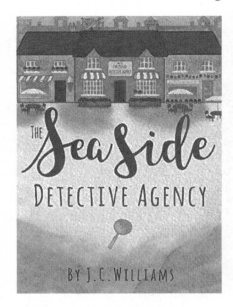

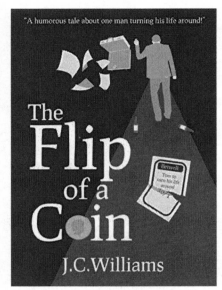

You may also wish to check out my other books aimed at a younger audience...

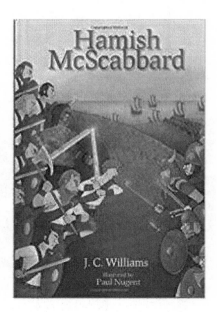

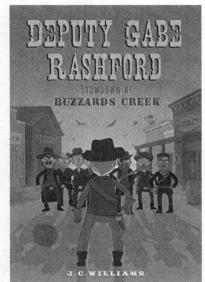

All jolly good fun!

And also…

For the *very* adventurous among you, you may wish to give my hardworking editor's most peculiar book a butcher's. Lavishly illustrated by award-winning artist Tony Millionaire of *Maakies* and *Sock Monkey* fame.

Recommended for readers age 14 and up.

Made in the USA
San Bernardino, CA
09 March 2020